SPRING BREAK

by Jon Waller

SPRING BREAK

JON WALLER

Kravitz & Sons
INNOVATORS IN PUBLISHING, MARKETING AND ADVERTISING

Kravitz and Sons LLC
1301 Farmville Blvd, Suite 104
Greenville, NC 27834

Published by Kravitz and Sons LLC.
ISBN: 979-8-89639-166-1 (sc)
ISBN: 979-8-89639-165-4 (e)

Library of Congress Control Number: 2025907471

Because of the dynamic nature of the Internet, any web addresses or links contained in this book may have changed since publication and may no longer be valid. The views expressed in this work are solely those of the author and do not necessarily reflect the views of the publisher, and the publisher hereby disclaims any responsibility for them.

Contents

This is dedicated to Barbara who has beenmy inspiration and rock and the love of my life.

Jon

PROLOGUE

Spring break in florida is a period of madness and exuberance when inhibitions run wild among the young adults visiting during school breaks in the spring of each year. Dancing and drinking to excess seems to be the norm, usually as a prelude or ritual to mating between consenting parties. A beach is often required to make these seasonal rituals click. But somewhere in florida spring break is a state of mind that knows no age limits and is not measured by the seasons. It is perpetual. There it is always "spring break."

CHAPTER ONE

THE GOLF MATCH

Coeur d'Alene Idaho Summer 2018

Brad Pope was in the shape of his life. He had trained steadily for the last two years for his first full Ironman triathlon, and he was determined to finish high in his age group category. Now approaching 59, he was going to age up and compete against competitors in the 60 to 65 age group. At an inch short of six feet and weighing in at a little under 170, he could push his body and endure the pain that just came with the sport of triathlon. While the training could fight off the aging of the body, it had not prevented his black hair from turning silver. Well, at least it was still there. In truth he knew that this sport was hard on his body, and it was taking longer to recover from the long workouts required by the event.

Fortunately, his career with the Secret Service required him to remain fit and he had come to the sport with high expectations. But this sport of triathlon was very unforgiving and humbling. He had worked hard and now he felt he was ready to try the first full length Ironman race. Would he be able to do it? The doubt would be as big a hurdle as the distance. After he and his wife Kate had checked into the Resort at Coeur d'Alene, he wanted to look over the course and in particular the swim course.

This race had all the traditional components of a full Ironman distance competition: a 2.4 mile swim, a 112 mile bike ride, and topped off by a 26.2 mile run. It would be a grueling day, but if he

1

could just get through the swim, the day would start off on the best of footing. Standing on the bank of Lake Coeur d'Alene, he could feel the icy waters from where he stood. The day before the race he would take a practice swim and see how cold it really was and whether he had made the biggest mistake in his life signing up to compete in this race. As the tension built up, he knew he needed to spend the day in a way to release the knots in his gut and to spend the day with his wife, Kate. Kate had put up with so much just to help Brad get to this race that she needed some time before the race to chill out. While the ambience of the resort town was magnificent and somewhat of a reward for Kate, Brad knew what would really make her jump for joy would be a round of golf at the renowned Coeur d'Alene Resort Golf Club. It was famous for its floating island green and had hosted many regional and national events over the last two decades. And Brad was right. She had leapt for joy when he mentioned that he had booked tee times for them three days before the race. She had had time to pack her trusty Callaway clubs and was really looking forward to the outing. Brad knew that watching her crush the ball down the fairways and putt the ball with uncanny accuracy would pale in comparison to how she would fill out the new golf dress she had packed for the trip.

Kate was the love of Brad's life. They had been high school sweethearts and had married while Brad had attended law school. Kate, with her blonde hair and high cheekbones and blue eyes that would just knock you out with a stare, was a perfect match for Brad. Her support and love had driven Brad throughout his career. He was her protector, and she reinforced his need to be a preserver of the high moral ground.

Brad had wanted to get to the race venue several days in advance so that he could ease into the event with low anxiety, and a round of golf would do that and would be a good way to thank Kate. So later that morning, three days before the race, they got on a motorboat from the CDA Resort and sped off for a thirty-minute ride to the Golf Club. The concierge had advised them that it was actually easier to travel by high-speed boat across the lake than to drive the rent car through town and over the rolling hills to the Club. Besides, it was a great way for Brad to survey part of the swim course and to gauge how cold the water was. And was it ever cold. The air temperature was already 75 degrees when they walked out of the Resort but felt nearly 20 degrees colder on the boat. Kate was really glad they had taken up the concierge's recommendation to wear pants and sweatshirts and a sweater. While she had her gorgeous blond hair in a ponytail, she had a warm hat pulled over her head. If it warmed up, she said she could always remove the warm gear. Brad and Kate had played many golf courses in the last few years as preparation for Brad's planned retirement from the Secret Service. He had been focusing on a retirement date in the fall of that year. He had heard of the various bucket lists that his colleagues had constructed and knew that golf and triathlons were high on their lists. He had decided to try both rather than choose. Kate was quite an athlete in her day, and although she was a fairly good swimmer and biker, her knees were not built for running. So triathlons were out for her, but golf was definitely a shiny lure.

One of the unique features of the golf course was an island green. Not like the one you see at the Player's Championship in Ponte Vedra, Florida, but truly an island that floats about 100 yards offshore. The island is in reality a barge that is well landscaped and can be moved inward towards shore or further out into the lake depending on the desires of the local golf pro. Access to the green is by motor launch piloted by an employee of the club. The green does tend to rock a little if the wind is very strong, but putting is quite true. Kate had read up on this unique feature of the golf course and was looking forward to the golf.

Brad and Kate signed in, charging the rounds to their resort room, and walked through the dressing rooms and out to the carts. There they were introduced to their playing partners, Duke and Robin Davidson. Duke was the General Manager of a famous new golf and country club in Fort Myers, Florida, called River Palms Golf and Country Club. They were staying at the CDA resort as well and attending a convention of managers of golf clubs from Florida. They seemed quite nice, but Brad and Kate knew they were not going to bet on the outcome of the match when the Assistant Pro checking them in at the first tee mentioned to them that Duke was a former touring pro and that Robin had recently beaten the assistant golf pro at River Palms in match play.

Duke was probably in his forties, guessed Brad. He was over six feet and, if Brad had to guess, a little north of 185 pounds. His hair was black like Brad's had been in his youth. But there were a few streaks of grey at the temples that could be seen under his golf cap. Robin looked half his age and was wearing a golf outfit that could be seen on some of the touring women professionals on the LPGA that did not mind showing off their full figures. This one was tight enough to make an adult film actress blush. It did not inhibit her golf swing a bit as Brad could attest after the round.

Brad suggested that the guys share a cart and that the gals take the other so that they all could get better acquainted. When Duke suggested they play from the Black Tees, Brad demurred and chose the shorter white tees. Kate stood on the first tee and knew that her first drive would be good because a beautiful iridescent yellow butterfly landed on her ball. She backed off and was reminded of a friend she had recently lost to cancer. Butterflies are a sign of good luck her friend had always said to her. Kate was pretty sure she would have the round of her life no matter how good this Robin was.

It was pretty even from the tee box for all the golfers, but Brad's iron game was definitely rusty. Kate, though, was pounding the ball, and on the greens she was a demon. She did have the round of her life. Her tee shot to the famed island green was a kick in birdie, while Brad lost two to the water. When they had finished the round, Kate was walking on air because Robin had barely beat her. Brad was happy to break 100. Duke, who shot in the low seventies, suggested they stay for lunch, adding that they had a good menu of burgers and heart healthy dishes. Brad and Kate could not say no. Walking to the Clubhouse after the round, they noticed the color of the water was a blue that they had only seen when they were visiting the island of Capri. Brad and Kate saw a few massive pinecones dotting the cart path and kicked one to the other. This was a wonderful day.

At lunch, Brad explained they were there for the Ironman triathlon and he planned to compete. Kate was his main support and cherished her role as Brad's Sherpa, or official assistant. Duke asked if the race was that Sunday. Yes, Brad told him, in three days. Duke said he and Robin would like to cheer for Brad and help Kate if that was OK. Brad said the more support and cheering the better. Kate knew all the best places to watch the race, and they agreed to meet her on Sunday morning at the start of the swim. Kate said all the swimmers were in black wetsuits, so it would be impossible to identify Brad. She said she usually just stood near the swim start and screamed as loudly as she could for Brad. She knew he could probably not hear her voice at all.

Duke then asked if he had heard the Golf Resort assistant pro right when he introduced Brad as a Secret Service Agent. Brad confirmed the information and said he was currently using his accumulated leave time and vacation before his retirement date became official. Duke asked Brad what he intended to do in retirement besides play golf and compete in triathlons? Well, Brad told him, he was talking with a few firms about security work, but nothing definite had matured so far. He had a headhunter shopping his resume. Duke asked Brad if he could e-mail it to him when he got a chance.

Chapter Two

The Race: Body Versus Mind

The day before the race, Brad went for a practice swim in the lake. He had anticipated that the water would be cold as the lake was mountain fed. He wore the wetsuit in which he planned to race. He even had a head cover that was made of a rubber material. The rules permitted him to wear booties because the water temperature was less than 65 degrees. Only his face and hands were uncovered. But when his face hit the water, he felt that he had been slapped on both cheeks. The cold was shocking. He knew his swim strategy would have to be "get in, swim fast, and get out!" Someone he knew that had done the event the year before said she had to immerse her hands in a warm water pool after the swim before she could even change into her bike outfit. After he was in the water for 15 minutes, he knew this was going to be tougher than he thought.

After the swim, he checked on the mechanics of his bike and dropped off both his biking and running clothes and made sure he had not left anything out of the bags. He would bring his nutrition and fluids Sunday morning. Before he left, he walked around the transition area where the bicycles were set up on racks and observed that with twenty-five hundred competitors and the average bike with advanced wheels and computers costing about $4,000, the competitors had at least $10,000,000 invested in the bikes, maybe more. Of course, the professional athletes were riding $15,000 to $20,000 bikes. His $500 bike would get his body around the course eventually, and it would have to do.

Early to bed after a light meal, sleep did not come easy nor was lengthy. Brad stirred around 3 am Sunday and made a light breakfast. He got dressed in his swimsuit and warm morning attire, mixed his special drink concoction, brushed his teeth, used the bathroom one last time, kissed Kate good morning, grabbed his wetsuit and timing chip and left for the transition area. There he loaded his bike with all the right liquid he would need for the first leg of the bike race and put the rest in the halfway, or special needs, bag, checked his bike again, and put on the wetsuit and googles. The chaos was just starting. Some of the guys were calling out for new timing chips to put on their ankles as they had forgotten theirs, others were screaming out for extra goggles, and one or two were finding out that the wetsuits they had brought from home did not fit as well as they had twelve months ago or that the zipper was broken and did not work. Obviously, they had not practiced a swim the day before to check out these major items they needed. In this race the competitors would all start en mass after the professionals were about a quarter of a mile in front. Brad and the other swimmers had been permitted to do a brief warm up in the water, but he was afraid it would just be counterproductive. He did walk to the water's edge and splash water on his face and get his bootie clad feet wet. As the pros started and the sky brightened a bit, he gazed around the boat dock and spotted Kate in a bright outfit. Duke and Robin were standing next to her. Brad knew with twenty-five hundred people dressed in various shades of black that they had no idea where he was. He turned his attention to the pros who were well along the first leg of the swim course. Then the gun went off signaling for the rest of the field to start, and the mad dash for the water began.

The swim of an Ironman length race is 2.4 miles. The swim course is typically set up either as a point to point or a two or three lap event. all marked with bright inflated buoys. Coeur d'Alene is a two-lap swim with competitors getting out after lap one and running about one hundred yards before getting back in to finish the second lap. Many just walked back to the hotel after failing to finish lap one or opting not to continue with the second lap.

Kate had positioned herself strategically on the dock overlooking the swim start and had skillfully pulled Duke and Robin through the crowd of spectators to a prime position. As she knew from her Sherpa duties in other races, it would be nearly impossible to pick out Brad among all the black wetsuits. At best she could differentiate between the women with their pink bathing caps and the men with their green caps. But that was it. She was hoping to see him running along the beach between laps one and two. The mountain-fed air was quite chilly as she looked at the swimmers moving from the start towards the middle of the lake. Then she saw something unusual for an Ironman swim. Numerous townies had revved up their boats and jet skis and had gathered near the turnaround point of the swim and were engaged in synchronized spin maneuvers. The relatively calm lake was churning now, waves hitting the swimmers as they neared the turn. While they were not so close to the turn as to create a hazard, the wave action was not what the swimmers needed after a half mile of a swim in ice cold waters. Fumes from the crafts drifted back to the dock area, causing Kate and her crew to choke and their eyes to water. She was irate as she knew Brad and the others would certainly not be breathing the fresh air they had planned to be taking in with each swim stroke. She learned that this was a race tradition for the townies and would continue until they were shoed away by the race officials. All Kate could do was bite her lip and shake her head in disbelief. Finally, as the swimmers had made the first turn, the crafts were shoed away, and the air began to clear.

Brad managed to get through the first lap despite the gasoline and diesel fumes and moved on to lap two. He no longer had to zig and zag on lap two as fewer swimmers were near him on this lap. He then caught his rhythm and followed more closely to the buoys and finished in under two hours by his reckoning. Kate and the crew spotted him emerging from the lake just as the announcers were calling out each swimmer over the loudspeaker. They thought he looked OK moving from the sand to the transition area where he would change. Brad warmed up in the change tent and put on his bike outfit and found his bike, ran it to the bike start, climbed on, and set off on a 112 mile Sunday bike ride. He saw Kate in her bright race day sweat suit at the bike start, but he was so focused on mounting the bike that he did not even wave.

The bike course was a two loop ride with two climbs with nearly sixty-five hundred feet of elevation. Basically, it was biking up one side of a mountain and down the other and then back again twice. It was one of the toughest bike courses in the US. And if one did not hydrate adequately on the bike, it would spell trouble on the run. Brad cruised through the 112 mile bike course in about six hours. Now the race would really begin.

Brad spotted Kate's crew as he emerged from the change tent and confidently began the 26.2 mile run. The run course was somewhat hilly and had some generous shade that made the roads cooler than other Ironman races. But what is described as a run with rolling or moderate hills in the race brochure is in reality a mountainous course to the participants. Why? They have just completed a two hour swim and a six hour bike ride over a mountain

Every time that he saw Kate and the cheering Davidsons, it boosted his spirits and drove him on the run. But his body would dominate his willpower. His chest began to hurt after about 10 miles. Walking seemed to help initially, but the pain persisted. He struggled to mile fifteen and decided that the pain probably was related to the stents that had been placed in his heart a few years before. He walked towards a medical tent and was grabbed by a volunteer and placed in an ambulance and taken to Kootenai Medical Center.

CHAPTER THREE

Kate: A Sherpa At Work

It was six P.M. and Kate knew that Brad had made the transition from bike to run, and she was planning to meet him at mile fifteen which he would eventually pass if things worked according to plan. Brad always mapped out his schedule for Kate before every race so that she could walk to each meet point and cheer him on. Usually his predictions turned out just about on time. Duke and Robin were going back to the resort to wait. They had plenty of time to catch dinner and bring something for her to the finish line bleachers. Ironman had set up a big screen that showed each finisher running down the red carpet to the finish line. She had seen him finish nine times in shorter races, all on flat warm courses, and was looking forward to seeing him cross the finish line here at Coeur d'Alene. She could hear the cowbells now clanging from the finish bleachers. It was at least a mile back there, but according to Brad's plan, she would have plenty of time. She had decided not to rent or buy a chair to carry from point to point as it was a pain to carry even a lightweight chair all over the racecourse. So she sat down on the roadside curb. It was now near 6:15 P.M. Hmmm. Where was he? Could she have missed him? Passing the marker were marines carrying colors and the flag, police officers dressed in uniform and running shoes, and a fireman in full gear and boots along with other racers, men and women at various stages of exhaustion.

She thought to call the Davidsons and give them an update. Oops, no phone. She had left it in the room. How many times did Brad tell her to take her phone with her? She walked back to the hotel, planning then to go to the finish line. She always put some bathroom stops in her route, and the hotel was usually the first choice for an experienced Sherpa. When she was about to leave the room, having picked up her cell phone, the hotel room phone rang. She answered the phone and said, "Hello."

The woman on the line asked, "Have you heard from your party?"

"What party? Who is this?"

"Your husband walked into the medical tent and was transported to the Kootenai Medical Center." Instantly Kate's knees buckled. She collapsed to the floor almost dropping the phone.

"Where is he now?" she asked.

The woman said, "He is in the emergency room." She hung up and called Duke and Robin. He located the Medical Center on his phone, and he said he would drive.

If you know how congested it is around an Ironman, getting out of the center of the action to a hospital requires serious driving. Most of the roads were blocked, but of course, the ambulance did made it. So had Duke. Upon arriving at the Medical Center, Kate was advised by the ER receptionist that the Kootenai Medical Center was one of the best hospitals in the country. She waited along with Duke and Robin. Kate was told that Brad was fine and being released. She was told that the process had been so quick because the ER doctor on duty was the head of cardiology and had been at the race working the medical tent just a few hours ago. He had taken a special interest in Brad and pushed the lab for all the results. He met with Kate and said, "From the tests results, there was no heart attack or heart related issue but that Brad was severely dehydrated. He took three bags of saline and was feeling fine and was being released."

When Brad came out to the waiting room, he said he was feeling great. He was talking about returning to the race. He said he had time to finish, and he still had his timing chip on his ankle. Kate popped Brad on the back of his head saying, "Stop it, you are not going to finish anything. Get in the car. Sleep is what you are going to do, not run!" Brad said that he had to return his chip and get his gear and bike out of transition and up into the room before midnight. Duke looked at Robin and said they would take care of it and took the claim ticket for the race gear and bike.

After Brad was released, Duke drove them back to the CDA resort. While Duke went for the race gear and bike and turned in the chip, Brad sat in his room and listened to the last hour of the race finishers cross the finish line. Hearing the Ironman announcer, Mike O'Reilly, shout, "You are an Ironman," over 500 times during the last hour of the race was almost more than Brad could take. With each call and corresponding cheer, Brad sat there shaking his head. He got up every now and then and saw the big screen at the finish line from their room. He could see finisher after finisher joyfully cross the finish line. Brad's mood shifted from guilt to sorrow to anger and then to acceptance. Then he decided he would do another race if Kate would be there for him. He resolved that Coeur d'Alene would not have the last word in his Ironman career. Kate listened to him agonize over his performance and offered solace as best she could. She had been a good Sherpa; she knew what to say. She said that she would be there for him if and when he would do another race. Duke and Robin returned his gear and bike around midnight, reporting they had wandered around in total darkness in transition looking for his gear bags and bike, but they completed the mission.

Duke and Robin saw Kate in the lobby the next morning as she was carrying coffee upstairs to Brad. Duke offered his condolences to Brad saying that he knew how much finishing had meant to him. Kate thanked him for his well wishes. Duke suggested a lunch if Brad was up to it. Kate said she would suggest that Brad do it if he was feeling OK. Duke reminded Kate that Brad was going to share his resume with him. Kate said that she was sure he would. Robin said she hoped they would all see each other again. Lunch did not take place because Brad spent most of the day in bed, and Kate joined him, doing her best to console him. While he really needed sleep, he did not get much that day.

Brad and Kate returned home to Falls Church, a town in Northern

Virginia just south of the 495 Beltway of Washington, DC. It had been their home for the past 10 years. It was close to his office and proved to be a great place to raise their two girls and see them through college. Brad and Kate were flexible about retirement living, but being near their daughters was important. Many of his colleagues were retiring to Florida. If Duke contacted him, he certainly would go and see what he had to say, but he wondered what he could do consulting for a country club.

CHAPTER FOUR

Paradise: West Coast of Florida

Duke called several days after Brad and Kate got back to Virginia from the race. Duke was interested in insourcing the security for his club. The head of one of the developer's subsidiaries was handling security for the community, and Duke wondered whether Brad could come down and give some recommendations on how to make River Palms (RP) more secure. Brad said that he had some time on his hands as a result of accumulated leave and could come down in the next week. He said he would like to bring Kate along if that was OK. Duke was pleased and they agreed on a time. "Bringing Kate is a great idea," he said.

Brad asked Kate if she wanted to come with him on a trip to consult on security arrangements at Duke's club. She said, "A trip to Florida? Sounds great! Maybe we should look at some property there in case we really like it."

"I am not sure they are looking to offer me full time job, but looking never hurts," he said.

On the first of September, a Wednesday, they got a flight out of Dulles and flew directly to Fort Myers, rented a car, and drove to the RP community. Brad wanted to drive the perimeter of the Community before he entered it. Brad had done some research on the Community, which had been completed by the developer Sean Smith and Co. a few years before. The website said that RP and Smith still had a few issues to work out in the turnover. The Community was independent of Smith with its own board of directors elected by the owners. It had about two thousand residences with a variety of home styles: single family, duplexes, and multifamily structures, some with two and others with four stories. Each presented their own security issues. On the south edge of the property, a river, just a gently flowing stream really, ran towards the Bay. The Community had a boathouse and a launch point for small crafts that could reach the deeper waters of the Bay if desired. There were two golf courses, tennis, pickle ball facilities, a fitness center, a huge clubhouse with two ballrooms, a pub, a covered outdoor bar and grill and patio overlooking a huge family recreational pool, and an attached lap pool. This latter area was often called just the Pool Bar. The Clubhouse contained the Pro shops for golf and tennis, together with expansive locker rooms and spa facilities for men and women and the administrative offices of the Club. He learned from his investigation online that the Community had a few developer-owned properties. Some of the original owners inhabited their homes year-round. Others split their residence between RP and a place they owned or rented up North. Not many held their properties for rent to snowbirds or even to those looking for temporary housing. But this was changing with the economy as residents were purchasing additional units nearby to rent to friends or to offer over the internet. The attractiveness of owning investments that one could see and touch and control seemed more appealing than a money market fund with all the fees and vagaries of the stock market. The sign on the front gate should have had a subscript, "Investors looking for a quick buck should enter these gates." But of course it did not.

Both Brad and Kate were blown away by the appearance of the Community. Its buildings and landscaping were first class. The gate house entrance was grand and inviting. It was easy to see why the Community was creating a buzz throughout Fort Myers. Entering the Community through the front gate was a breeze as the gatehouse had been alerted to his appointment and waved them in. He noted that the attendant had not asked for any identification or captured any information as to his vehicle. He was handed a map of the Community and offered directions to the Clubhouse and the General Manager's office. Approaching the Clubhouse, both Kate and Brad observed that it was as elegant as some of the world class destinations they had visited such as the Greenbriar and the Cloisters. This was impressive, they agreed.

He parked the car and he and Kate walked up to the front door of the Clubhouse. At the front door, he was greeted by the Administrative Assistant to the GM, Janey Boothe, who suggested that after she showed Brad Duke's office, she should take Kate for a guided tour of the grounds in one of the Club's golf carts. Kate thought that was a better proposition than leaving Brad for a trip to the local Target store. Brad kissed Kate goodbye at the entrance to Duke's office and went in, leaving Kate to Janey's care.

Duke greeted Brad warmly and offered him a seat in what was an extremely spacious office. It had, in addition to the uncluttered executive style desk and computer, a large couch, a glass coffee table, and two matching club chairs squaring off the sitting area with a large overly stuffed leather, winged-back chair opposite the couch. In the corner of the office there was a mini shrine to the Masters, a pair of Palmer autographed shoes, and an Augusta Country Club golf bag with Duke's name monographed on the bag. Impressive. Brad had not seen such a large executive office outside of the State Department executive offices in DC. Duke poured him a cup of coffee and began to talk about security at RP.

The Security Plan which Sean Smith, the developer had approved, focused on protecting the construction equipment while it was present as well as the golf and fitness center. Many nonresidents routinely entered the property either as potential buyers of residences or users of the dining and recreational facilities, such as golf or tennis. The developer thought that it assisted its marketing and sales efforts. The contractor managing security for the Community was a subsidiary of the developer and run by the developer's daughter and son-in-law. Ralph Donald was the president in name but Sean Smith's daughter voted the shares. Even after the governance of the Community had been turned over to the owners, the contractor and its security protocols remained in place. Brad questioned Duke about areas of concern or incidents where the police department had to be brought onto the grounds. What followed was jaw dropping.

Duke explained that some of the first owners were a growing concern. The developer had informally marketed the property as a perpetual Spring Break Resort where owners could enjoy the good life, play hard, and party harder. The Community held nightly three for one drink specials, and Smith, mostly as a promotional gimmick, invited prospective purchasers to participate. The bar staff were instructed to "Keep them coming," and earned enormous tips and were happy employees, out earning most of the employees of bars and grills outside the Community. The revenues from the Pool Bar were so great that the owners were happy to see their annual dues so low. They were drinking themselves to lower dues, and the developer was selling homes hand over fist. After the developer met the criteria for completion and RP was turned over to the owners, management did adjust the ratio of drinks, but the interest in reining in alcohol consumption was not high on the Board's to-do list. Even with the number of free drinks cut back, the revenue from alcohol was over sixty percent of the food and beverage revenue. It drove the annual budget. Frequently, the residents would get carried away at the Pool Bar, and raised voices sometimes led to some pushing and shoving but nothing that required police intervention yet.

But bigger concerns were emerging. With the trend towards greater rentals, the internet was marketing the Community not only as a perpetual Spring Break but on some sites as a Club Med type of resort community. Swinging singles and large groups were being attracted to single dwellings. It was also being promoted as a great place for college kids to rent on a short-term basis for Spring Break, given how close the Community was to the beach. But many attracted to the Community saw it as a complete destination for fun and the sun. Food, booze, first class accommodations, golf, tennis, and a great nightlife with live entertainment at the right price: free! The Club's alcohol policy and the fabulous pools were a drawing point all year round. Many residents who owned and rented or owned multiple dwellings for rent wanted to find renters that had the same interests they did and that might view RP as a great place to become an owner themselves. They felt that those renting short term or to the so-called "Spring Breaker" type were potentially hurting the market price of homes in the community or at least affecting the reputation of the Community. But there were no firm restrictions on rentals that were binding on the owners. If the law permitted it, that was good enough.

Brad thought things might be worse than Duke would admit. He pointed out that if this was sold to owners as a gated community, there were some aspects of security that were not being addressed. "Like what?" Duke inquired.

Brad said, "The fence line did not extend completely around the community; the stream or river flowing along the south border had no fence line at all and permitted complete access from the waterway; there were no cameras or video capture of the front gate or pool areas." Brad pointed out that in the few places he had looked at, such as the bar area or access to the pro shops, nothing. "Things could be walking out the pro shop door and might just be counted as shrinkage. Heck, without video, owners and guests could be stealing merchandise and bringing it back for cash returns, claiming they lost the receipt. Studies show that out of all people, twenty percent will never steal, twenty percent probably will steal, and the remaining sixty percent will be influenced by how likely they will be caught. Candid Camera did several skits that confirmed this using planted wallets," Brad said. He added, "The front gate seemed to be more focused on getting the gate bar up and down than keeping uninvited guests out of the community." He asked if there had been any vehicles stolen from the residents. Duke admitted that there were about five cars a month that simply disappeared. The police investigated every one, but nothing was being solved. Brad pointed out that the fences were not very high and could easily be jumped, and if there was little or no surveillance, thefts as well as burglaries could be expected. Brad asked whether there was a log of all contractors kept and whether residences listed all people that came into their houses, such as cleaning or home watch personnel.

Duke sat in silence nodding. He then said, "Brad, it would be very helpful if you would agree to spend a few days here and help me evaluate what we need to do to minimize the risks we face and the steps we need to protect the Community." He continued, "I think you would be a perfect fit as our Security Director, but if you would at least do this consulting job, I would appreciate it."

Brad said, "I can give you a week, but I have no place to stay as I was expecting to fly home this evening."

Duke said Janey was showing Kate a furnished house that the Club repossessed from an owner that was available for the foreseeable future which they could have rent free. He said, "The Club will also extend dining privileges to you both during your stay. I can offer you a contract at $500 a day plus expenses and access to our fitness and aquatic facilities so you can do some training while you are here. There are, by the way, some excellent biking and running routes, if you have not already scouted them out."

Brad said, "Let's get started."

Duke reached into his top desk drawer and pulled out a folder, opened it up, and slid it over to Brad. It was a one-page contract that Duke told him had been approved by the Board President, Stosh Salinski, that morning. It called for a consulting fee of $500 per day, free housing and meals, unlimited free access to the amenities of the Club, and reimbursement of expenses. Brad signed it, put it in the folder, and slid it back to Duke. Brad followed Duke out the back door of the Clubhouse and they got into a golf cart and off they went. Brad spoke to Duke and said, "You know this missing car thing is costing residents of RP $100,000 to $200,000 a month? This is a big-time theft ring, and I will give that immediate priority."

They drove around the perimeter of the property both inside and outside, walked the fence line and around the auxiliary gates, the maintenance facility, and the outside access to it from a back road; walked through the cart barn where golf carts and equipment were stored; and stopped and asked some of the cart personnel whether any carts were missing and whether they could be tracked in real-time. They walked through the clubhouse, including the kitchen and all the bar facilities, Brad paid particular attention to the areas where ADA required and recommended facilities should be installed. He said that he wanted to talk with the facilities director to follow-up on the ADA requirements as well as fire suppression devices and equipment. He also wanted to spend some time with the golf and maintenance directors to go over their protocols and safety and security policies. He also wanted to meet informally with the key board members, particularly those on any health and safety committees as well as the Audit Committee members. If those folks could be lined up in the next week, he felt it reasonable to complete the work for a report within a week. Duke said between he and Janey, it would happen.

Kate and Janey got back to the Clubhouse and had lunch with Duke and Brad. Kate described the house they went through and how much she liked it. It was beautifully decorated and furnished. Brad said, "Glad you like it because we will be spending the next week in it while I work on a security plan for the Club if you are willing to stay for a while."

"Oh that would be great." she said. "I guess I should do some shopping while you start to work." Janey handed her the keys to the home and showed Brad an office and a computer station where he could begin his work. Some of his meetings had been set up for the afternoon.

As Kate was leaving in the car, Brad mentioned to her he wanted to get to the beach and get in a swim before it got dark. She winked and said she would be back to pick him up at five P.M. As she was pulling out of the parking lot, a driver blew through a stop sign and sped out of the Community at an excessive speed. Brad thought, "What am I getting into?"

At five P.M. sharp Kate picked up Brad and drove down to the beach. He sat in the passenger seat of the convertible they had rented and stared at her tight fitting bikini and white ball cap. "I guess you did not get that outfit at Target. The royal blue goes with your eyes." She laughed and said his swim gear was in the trunk. The route to the beach went through avenues of stately palm trees, beautifully landscaped neighborhoods, a causeway that spanned a large body of water with sand covered islands dotted with magnificent palm trees and filled with sun seekers catching the final hours of sunlight clustered across the sand. Pelicans and seagulls swept over the causeway in the gentle breeze, moving up and down, looking for food the beach goers might have left unguarded or a fish that swam too close to the surface of the Bay. This was the Bay that the river from RP emptied into. They arrived at the jewel of an island called Sanibel and found a perfect beach with public parking and change facilities. Brad quickly changed and hit the beach and the water. What a change from the ice-cold waters of that Idaho lake. The water temperature of Sanibel was warmer than seventy-six degrees, and it felt soothing to glide through the water parallel with the beach. Kate followed along, walking the beach. As he swam north, he could see her every other stroke, breathing on his right side. He almost wanted to stop every time he spotted the royal blue bikini. God, he was so lucky to have her. After a forty-five-minute swim, Brad got out of the water, toweled off, sat with Kate, and they watched the sun go down. It was a spectacular sunset. After dinner at the Island Manatee, they returned to RP and Kate somehow found the house in the dark.

Chapter Five

Is Spring Break Broken:
Escape From The Winter

In the early days of Florida's development, there were no superhighways criss-crossing the state. But there were beautiful ports of call for yachts and steamers that connected inaccessible parts of Florida with northern states and even cities along the Mississippi River. Industrialist, inventor, and celebrity Thomas Edison made a strategic decision to acquire land in the small town of Fort Myers on the Caloosahatchee River. He had explored sites in Florida by steamship and decided it would be an ideal site to escape the harsh winters of New Jersey and New York. He immediately established a laboratory. With Fort Myers's access to the Gulf of Mexico, exotic plants that might further his research into filaments for light bulbs, synthetic rubber, and other inventions were imported. The lab attracted Edison's employees and inventors from Menlo Park in New Jersey as well as industrialists Henry Ford and Harvey Firestone who also built homes along the Caloosahatchee River in Fort Myers. On the east coast of Florida, developers were completing a rail line to the south of Florida. Notably, Henry Flagler, also head of Standard Oil, financed a great portion of the railways and established large destination hotels, which were marketed to upper class residents in Northern Cities as the destination to escape the bitter cold of winter and enjoy the early spring weather. And they came to both coasts.

Following WWII, the expansion of the National Highway system provided important access to the beaches of Florida. Annual Spring events were organized, such as Daytona car racing. Popular moving picture shows centered around the beautiful beaches of the east coast of Florida. College students were hooked and began flocking to the newly constructed strip motels. Mid-Western colleges, Northeastern colleges, and even Southern colleges began spacing out their winter and spring breaks to accommodate requests from Florida cities to space out the overwhelming demands on the roads and then in the air as air transportation began to supplement the mad rush for Florida. As grandparents and parents rushed to snap up newly constructed gated homes and condos, children and grandchildren joined the annual migratory dash for warmer climates. Florida towns that resembled ghost towns in the off-season sprung to life in Winter and Spring. Grocery stores that failed to remove expired grocery items from the shelves in off months were receiving almost hourly truckloads of produce to stock the shelves. Super Walmarts and Targets have dotted the landscape in recent years to supply the frenzied demand for food and beach items.

Beaches were taken over by afternoon and evening beach parties, attracting young adults seeking alcoholic highs and brief interludes between thinly clad men and women. Beach bars that catered to local residents in the off season saw the opportunity to make a full year's profit in a short two months of Spring Break. The sheer volume of visitors overwhelmed any efforts to police underage drinking even if the beach communities desired to address the problem. But why would they. From a tax revenue perspective, sales generate tax revenue. The more alcohol and food sales, the more rooms that are rented, the more beach junk sold, and the lower assessments on residential real estate properties. Lower rates meant more votes at election time. Spring Break made voters happy until they were not.

Investors sought alternate ways to guarantee returns, particularly if beach front properties became scarce. Orlando had their theme parks after early risk takers like Walt Disney saw a future no one else did. Indian tribes won the right to develop casinos on land the courts determined had connection to Indian tribes or descendants of Indians. Investors began to gravitate to mega developments where anchor investors like retirees or those nearing retirement age could be lured to place much of their life savings in a luxury home or a seemingly inexpensive high rise condo that could easily be rented out to snow-birds and even spring breakers. But to sweeten the pot and secure greater returns for the developers and investors, they added sure fire amenities like championship golf courses, fantastic pools, enormous bars, and trendy fitness and spa centers. Make no mistake, the attractiveness of these communities also included the notion that life did not go on forever and that an active lifestyle included more than being fit for self-improvement but also the prospect of finding a future spouse, not that there is anything wrong with that. But look at the promotional materials objectively and you will see even in materials for 55+ communities, pictures of actors and actresses that are fifty-five rather than eighty-seven. Interestingly, one community in Florida leads the country in the occurrence rate of STDs, demonstrating that there is still an active sex life for grandparents, despite what the college kids might think. And communities like that one was more than fifty miles from the beaches of either coast. Resort style communities had arrived as tourist destinations sought out by non-college folks. Who needed beaches when we had all this?

Communities attempted to control the periodic rental of houses and condos in their new communities with policies and rules and covenants in their governing documents. It still required enforcement. More importantly, it required a unified commitment by owners to maintaining a community that was family oriented rather than one fostering an annual two-month orgy. Gone were the days when rentals were posted on a cork bulletin board and owners met and interviewed prospective renters. The internet had trashed all that. Speed, ease of reaching a large potential audience, handling of payments from credit cards, and scheduling overshadowed the intimacy of the past. It was big business with the property owner taking less and less of the pie. Spring Break mentality was an industry and God forbid anyone question its existence. But it was not a 365 day a year phenomenon. There were lulls created by weather. Northerners avoided the very hot summers. Who wanted to go to heat when it is hot in the North? Then tourists avoided the hurricane season, except the mad surfers seeking endless waves. So the real season would begin in the late fall and last until the summer. In just a month or so it would descend upon RP. Hopefully, the community would survive.

CHAPTER SIX

Loopholes: An Exciting Lifestyle

Alison Reynolds had recently filed for divorce from her husband Jake. Despite the advice of her divorce attorney, she remained in the same condo with her husband and three-year-old son Charlie. She knew Jake was good for her son Charlie and did not want to take Charlie permanently away from Jake. But she needed to get away while the dust settled. She had tired of the constant second guessing by her parents and Jake's. Why was a beautiful marriage on the rocks, they asked. You have a beautiful three-year-old boy; what more could you ask for? Are you being too inflexible; are you not giving Jake as much attention as he needs? Why are you still working that accounting job when Jake earns enough for you to stay home and raise your son? Is day care the right thing to be placing Charlie in? Do you need the fancy convertible when a Kia might do just as well? The final mandated marriage mediation with a marriage counselor was sixty days away, and she needed to just stop thinking about all the smoke that had built up from both sides of the family. Discussing the why's was too stressful. She wanted to get out and enjoy life, to party and meet interesting people. That would never happen as long as she stayed tied to Jake. Despite his good looks and being a good father to little Charlie, Jake was just boring. She was stifled; she needed some freedom, lots of freedom.

She found a website called "soyouwanttoparty.com" and began

to do her research. She found that the company was really named SYWTP, LLC and was incorporated in the British Virgin Islands to avoid taxes. The company would rent a property in an upscale resort-style community with lots of amenities and coordinate weekly or bi-weekly stays in the house or condo. Those interested would be asked to join a club, and membership would allow them to move from one community to another and to move from house to house within a community. This provided flexibility if a different living arrangement offered better or more exciting relationships. Members had to be unattached and interested in an active lifestyle. For those needing childcare, the club would offer one of the rental homes to handle that need, even if the need extended to overnight care. This sounded perfect. Allison downloaded the app, sent in a sexy picture (which the site required), and paid the entry fee. An hour later, the site contacted her and said she met the qualifications and was given a confirmation of her membership. As the website provided members with multiple resort style communities to choose from, Alison spent the weekend researching the communities and houses that members could occupy for a short-term basis. She could leave home with Charlie and take a great vacation in a resort that was not boring. Maybe she would find a real man that was interesting and not anywhere as ordinary as Jake.

When she found a destination that had everything on her checklist, she got out the credit card that she had recently gotten in the mail from the bank and became a "guest" of SYWTP, LLC for the next weekend, Thursday through Sunday afternoon. After receiving a confirmation, she received an address and an invitation for the first party of the week. She was told to bring a daring cocktail dress for the first evening. This was already starting to sound good.

Chapter Seven
The Guy She Left Behind:
What Did I Do Wrong?

Jake Reynolds had heard it in the first session of their mandated mediation: He was boring, no longer exciting, and Alison was just not interested in him. He loved her. and he loved Charlie. He was doing his best to provide a good life for them so that Alison would be able to stay home and raise Charlie as Jake had been raised. He was trying to better himself by attending business classes at the University at the Gulf. His work at the computer firm was intensive. and he devoted long hours to the job. His one quirk was that his interest in computers had introduced him to online gaming, and the one thing the mediator had gotten him to accept was that he was addicted to it. What he could not accept was that the addiction was a problem in the marriage because he believed it helped him not only at work but with his life survival skills. Maybe the mediator did have a point that he could defeat any computer game zombie that might be lurking in a closet, but he felt that the strategizing was a useful life skill. All the time spent working, gaming, and playing with Charlie meant less time at the gym. In fact he had let his membership lapse. He picked up weight and seemed less interested in his physical condition. Perhaps, he thought, he had just let himself go. Maybe a new exercise bike might help. Mediation clearly was not going to get Alison to be interested in their marriage. Maybe they needed something else to spark up the marriage. But what about "For better or worse"? They had it pretty good. Could it be that bad? Their condo was inland from the Gulf about 7 miles. They had underground monitored parking. The grounds had ample space for kids to play outside in good weather. There were walking trails and connecting bike paths to roads with designated bike lanes. There were schools in the vicinity of the condo complex, and when Charlie got older, he could walk to school. Life was good. Why was Alison complaining?

He got home early from work that Thursday night and went directly to the study and jumped on the home computer and logged onto his gaming account. He had not checked the condo to give Charlie a hug or Alison a curt "Hi". But after two hours, he began to get hungry and interrupted his game and went into the kitchen. It was dark, which confused him. He called out for Alison and Charlie, but they were just not home. He checked his phone and found a text message from Alison. It said, "I have to get out of here for a few days. I know things have to be more exciting out there than being stuck in this dumb condo. Taking Charlie. See you in a few days. A."

He sat down for a few minutes and said, "What the F***! Where is she? Where are they? How could she do this?" Maybe she was with her friend and staying there? "Just call her cell," he thought. So he did. It rang in the bedroom. She did not have it with her. "I cannot even track her on my phone app! And no dinner to boot!"

Chapter Eight

Party Central:

The House At River Palms

Alison and Charlie drove in the new convertible that Jake had leased for her. It was her favorite color, red, and had all the bells and whistles. She thought, "Maybe life is not as bad as I have been thinking." She had entered the address in her onboard computer, and the voice on the computer directed her turn by turn to the entrance of River Palms. She pulled up to the front gate and told the guard she was a guest of SYWTP, LLC at 11201 Martini Drive. The guard waved her through the gate after handing her printed directions. She waved as she and Charlie drove off for the Party House.

It was five P.M. when she arrived at the huge house at the end of the culdesac at the end of Martini Drive. It was a two-story house that swept around half of the culdesac. It had two entrances with a four-car garage connected to the house. The front door was open, and loud music with a great beat surrounded the house. She parked in the front of one of the garages, lifted Charlie out of his car seat, and set him on the ground. She reached in the trunk for her suitcases and walked to the front door, Charlie walking along with her. There, standing at the door was the President of SYWTP, Victor Vance. He said, "Hi, I'm Victor; you must be Alison Reynolds. What is this little guy's name?"

"This is Charlie, and he's three years old," she said. "I saw on the website that the house has facilities for Charlie to have his own quarters with professional care sitters," she added.

"Let me show you the quiet wing of the house and our sitter," said Victor. "This is Kaleisha Campbell. This is Alison Reynolds, and this is her son, Charlie. Alison, give your keys to Mason here," pointing to an attendant that just appeared.

She flipped the keys to the attendant and said, "After you, Victor," and followed Victor into the house. Victor paused halfway down the hall until Alison caught up to him. Victor gently reached around her and rested his arm on her shoulder as he said, "Alison, please call me Vic. Let me show you around before we escort Charlie to his quarters."

The house was two stories and shaped like a "U". In the center was a grand swimming pool under cover and, beyond, an enormous patio, which was surrounded by lights and hidden speakers carrying the music and booming to the beat. The pool could be entirely closed in by sliding glass that was a full two stories. The entrance hall opened up to a full kitchen and an enormous bar overlooking the living room/entertainment area. Upstairs rooms overlooked the pool area from a walkway. The master bedroom was on the right wing and contained a huge bar, a grand ensuite with a walk-in shower, a jacuzzi, and many other features that impressed Alison. The bed was an oversized King, which had a half moon window over the bed. There were large windows from which you could barely see the river that flowed by the RP Community along its journey to the Gulf. The other side of the second floor contained three bedrooms and a separate living space decorated for children. Back downstairs, they walked beyond the pool and onto the patio. Beyond the patio was a well-groomed yard that was landscaped beautifully with flowering shrubs and flowers. Vic said the owner had the plantings updated with the seasons so that the back yard was always blooming and full of color. A quartermile, tree lined path led to a landing from which canoes and kayaks could be launched and a dock from which small motorized crafts could be docked. This was a perfect getaway. Charlie seemed to like what he could see. The woods as well as the pool was an attraction that Kaleisha would have to be careful to keep Charlie from wandering too close to. Alison had a long talk with her. Kaleisha told her that she had come to Fort Myers from Kingston, Jamaica, with her husband and loved the area so much that she stayed. Her husband returned to Kingston, but she felt America was a good place to make a home. She was completing all her work for citizenship and was planning on being sworn in before Christmas. Alison felt comfortable with Kaleisha and gave her instructions about Charlie's peculiar eating and sleeping habits.

After she handed Charlie off to Kaleisha, she walked with Vic out to the pool. Vic leaned into her and lightly kissed her right shoulder. He told her that other guests would be arriving shortly and that he would deeply appreciate it if she would serve as the official hostess and show the guests around. She replied, "Sure Vic, it would be my pleasure," and he gave her a hug and a kiss on the cheek.

"Great, "he said. He told her that those who were staying would be assigned to one of the separate bedrooms at the house or in other houses that the company had rented for the month. This would be his version of a perpetual Spring Break for the guests. "We want to make the vacation a pleasurable experience for them all." She asked him which bedroom was hers, and he said, "Ours is the master bedroom, or if you are not comfortable with that, it is just yours." She looked at him briefly, grabbed a glass of champaign, and said, "Let the fun begin," adding, "I am sure we will enjoy the master bedroom tonight."

Chapter Nine

Vic: The Business Model

Vic was a fit, good looking guy; at least that is what Alison thought. He was a shade under six feet tall with dark brown eyes and reddish blond hair, the shade you see on actors. It was styled in a Nick Nolte kind of way that seemed to excite some women. Compared with Jake's receding hairline, it looked fantastic to Alison. Nearing forty, Vic had attended two years of junior college, leaving for a career in modeling and attempts to break into the acting field. He always seemed to find a way to duck the hard path and had a gift of gab that would persuade the stingiest of people to part with their money. If a venture sounded like a scam, Vic was probably involved. Sometimes he had great ideas and little capital to get the ideas off the ground. He was usually good at taking big risks with other people's money. He had convinced another developer, Fast and Luxurious, LLC (F&L) to build luxury homes next to the highly successful Ocean Palms Community just after taking an option on the land and flipping it to F&L. In return, F&L had agreed to build him the premier home in the new Palm Tree Reserve Community. However, he had had to commit to it being the model home for a year and buy the furnishings at the end of the year. His total investment for a home that would list in Palm Tree Reserve for $1.2 Million furnished was $10,000, which he borrowed. But that scheme was nothing compared to the party business concept. He knew from the business plans of many of the Florida home builders that marketing properties to prospective buyers suggesting rental opportunities worked much better for condos and apartment-like dwellings but not too well with single-family homes, particularly those that were on the higher end of the luxury curve. So he made a pitch a few years before River Palms was opened to the developer Smith to commit to leasing a minimum of thirty percent of the luxury homes, furnish them, and participate in the developer's marketing effort to sell these furnished homes to owners not ready to occupy the homes but interested in getting into a first-class neighborhood on the ground floor. If a sale was made, Vic would share in the proceeds, receiving a marketing fee. Until the sale, Vic's company would have full privileges to the RP facilities, gate privileges, and the understanding that guests of Vic could use the facilities as if they were members. Those guests could play golf, tennis, recreate at the pools, sign chits at the Pool Bar, and use the spa and fitness facilities. A prospective purchaser could either take full possession of the purchased home or opt to continue the lease arrangement for months the owner was not in possession. That was a straight-forward concept that did not turn off most future purchasers. Some were happy to get some rental income when they were not occupying the house. The fact that they got the furnishings for a song usually enhanced the deal. Except for a few houses that the developer retained subject to leases, the community was fully sold out and quickly. The homes were splendidly furnished, and the guests that occupied the homes subject to leases were predominantly the same age and fit well into the party scene at RP.

But Vic wanted more. He thought of ways to make more money off the top of even this incredible deal. First, he went to a number of high-end furnishing stores and interior decorators and offered the same deal developers were doing: Furnish the home at no cost to Vic, and he would invite countless prospective buyers in to see the beautiful home and your furnishings, your signage, and your marketing literature. So he would fully satisfy the obligation to Smith and would furnish the homes with high-end pieces. These properties would be open to potential buyers at the developer's open house program. If Vic was using them for his guests to sublet, he would remove them from the open house schedule. If the home designer or furniture store derived a sale from customers going through the open house that Vic had furnished, he would then receive a commission. If the house sold with the furnishings he had arranged, both the developer and the furniture store would pay him a commission. This cost him nothing but was simply another way to maximize his return. When a community like RP was fully sold out, he had another scheme, and this one would require him to drive a truck through the loopholes the developer was making with the new owners. He had surfed the internet and found that the rental market for vacation homes was big business. He would approach new purchasers of these estate homes and enter into rental arrange ments for the times they were not in occupancy, lease them up, and turn them into short term rentals. But there was more to be had. Monthly deals were the norm for the snowbird renter. Yet many of these snowbirds were thrifty and had been doing this for a long time. Many were asking for rental concessions for long term rentals of two or three months. Some were only interested in January and February with less interest in March. The most difficult were those that wanted only March, leaving the lessor with marketing January and February together or separately. The market value of the monthly or seasonal leases was driven by the interest in SWFL as a whole with premiums for homes with beach access. Renters of this type tended to be retirees or those testing the retirement waters. Renters of luxury homes off-beach were also driven by the idea of golf course amenities, but he saw the monthly rental market limiting. Vic felt that even shorter rentals might generate greater revenues, and that would be particularly true if he would market to a younger market rather than retirees. If you could attract a younger set of clientele, perhaps not with as much time on their hands, and lure them with a resort lifestyle, maybe even a party lifestyle, it might be different story. He toyed then with marketing a shorter rental period, perhaps a long weekend. He could create a whole new market. But maybe there was more. What if you created a swinging singles club that through membership had access to these luxury homes set in a resort style community with water access. It would be kind of a Party Club; you could have a party central house and entertain the guests in an over-the-top fashion. If the singles hooked up, a good buzz would be created. If you did all the marketing online with the payments passed through the website, there was unlimited potential until the neighborhood matured. Then he would move on to the next cash cow. So you want to party or SYWTP, LLC was born. That was three years ago, and Vic could not believe his bank account. He was viewed as mover and a shaker in Fort Myers. Not only that but he could not believe how many beautiful women he had met through SYWTP. Brief relationships with no strings were an attraction.

Alison appeared to be one of these women: young, beautiful, and searching for something else in life. It mattered little to Vic that she was stepping out on a marriage or that she had a young child. It made any relationship less likely to be a longterm one. She would just be another notch in his gun, another picture for his Postbook account. The house he picked as his party central was perfect for him to select a new companion, however briefly. He had designated it the Party House, and it was well known throughout Fort Myers.

Alison proved to be a great hostess that night. The guests arrived in five stretch limos, each filled with eight beautiful women. The men had arrived shortly after Alison had taken up her hostess duties. Valets moved cars from the house to the Club's large parking lot. More money for Vic as he shared the tips the valets earned. Some of the direct reports of the General Manager also arrived. Three key directors of RP arrived: Chip Bogatus, Frank Renquist, and Marvin Northcross also sauntered in. Even the developer and builder of RP, who was a regular visitor to the Party House, was present. The music blasted out over the pool and in the direction of the river, which helped keep the complaints down from the neighboring houses in RP. The female guests averaged thirty in age and were decked out in slinky evening wear that would make dancing and drinking easy and comfortable. The stretch limos were a brilliant stroke of genius. They were typically booked on the weekends for weddings and proms but not very active during the week. They were cheaper than a cab. He had arranged the limos to pick up some of the women from the local Walmart parking lots, some from their homes, and others from the guest houses in RP. Emerging from the stretch limos, they could make a grand entrance to the Party House and join the fun. They paired up with the available men and hit the open bars.

The party had continued to two A.M., and the Gatehouse recorded twenty irate phone calls from RP residents complaining about the loud music and laughing. No security vehicles came to visit the Party House, although a few calls were made to Vic from the Gatehouse requesting he turn it down a notch. Under Kaliesha's care, Charlie and the other children of the single parents taking advantage of the childcare services slept through the party. Alison had checked in on him before midnight, and he was sleeping deeply. By two-thirty A.M., the limos left with all that were not booked into the Party House or had hooked up with another guest in an available room. Alison was having such a great time she hardly noticed the time and almost missed Vic's hints to turn down the lights and let the cleaning crew take care of the party mess in the morning. He reached out his hand and said, "Come upstairs and let's get better acquainted. The night is still young. We can sleep in and go over to the Clubhouse for brunch with Charlie." She grabbed his hand, and they walked slowly up to the master bedroom. She thought, "This is not a boring guy, and I love his hair."

Chapter Ten

Brad: The Study

Friday morning Brad got in a five-mile run on the bike path outside the front gate. He found a younger runner doing sprints between long jogs. He chose not to join the workout. It was great running in a sleeveless tank top after all his runs in Northern Virginia in sweats this winter. He showered, grabbed a cup of Joe, and walked to the Clubhouse, leaving Kate with the car. She said she might go shopping for one of those sexy golf outfits that Robin had worn in Coeur d'Alene. He told her to get two.

He went into the Security director's office and asked Ralph Donald's secretary for a copy of all the Gatehouse reports for the last 30 days and returned to the office Janey had designated as his for the duration of the consulting role. He spent an hour interviewing the facilities director Rod Gomez, spending time on issues like posted speed limits, speed minders, video cameras, and maintenance equipment as well as fence maintenance as a first pass on facilities issues and contracts with suppliers. Rod was very knowledgeable with ten years of experience in the industry. He had held a comparable position in the last two developments that the builder had completed. His next appointment was with the security director, Ralph Donald. He had been briefed by Duke that Donald was the President of a wholly subsidiary of the builder. Brad knew that Duke had Donald and his firm in his cross sights, but he wanted to give him a fair assessment. Donald's security firm was working under a three-year contract that extended beyond the turnover of the Community to the owners. But there was a termination clause giving either party the right to terminate upon sixty days's notice.

Donald's background was as an assistant golf professional in golf courses that the builder had built in the last 10 years. Five years before, the builder had asked Donald to fill in on security duty at another community. His performance there was satisfactory, and he was brought over to handle security at RP. While he had taken courses at the local community college in law enforcement, it had not hurt that he had fallen in love with the developer's daughter and married her.

Brad said he wanted to get a measure of the man and his grasp of security issues. He told Donald that he wanted to spend just a short time before lunch talking security issues. He asked Donald to list the three key security issues on his plate in the last month. These might be driven by frequency of occurrence or degree of risk. Donald paused a bit and said, "OK, here they are off the top of my head: a) the lack of clear rules regarding conduct of owners and staff; b) our cars, we don't know who cars belong to; we cannot prevent owner's cars from being stolen; the cars are parked wherever they want; the cars speed through the community; and the cars that enter the community are not tracked adequately to determine when they leave; c) the party atmosphere that pervades the community and disturbs the quiet enjoyment by owners and guests."

"Quite a list," observed Brad. "You have given this a bit of thought. Have you had an opportunity to address these issues with the Board of Directors?"

"No. I think that little I suggest will be well received by the Board as they have their minds made up on some of these issues and generally dismiss my views as a vestige of the developer. I understand that, and frankly, I'm glad Duke has brought someone in to help address some of these issues and provide a fresh set of eyes and spot any other issues that might be of equal concern."

"What is an example of ideas that the Board may have made their mind up?" Brad asked.

"Well let's take a look at the write-ups from last night," Donald said. "There was a huge party last night on Martini Drive, with loud music and stretch limos. We had multiple complaints to the Gatehouse about the noise, and per instructions from the GM, at the direction of the Board to simply contact the homeowner and ask them to cut back on the noise. That was how it was handled," he said. "We have no way of enforcing any conduct that interferes with the enjoyment of peace and quiet of a neighbor after a reasonable hour. These calls came in between midnight and 2 AM," he said. "This is Spring Break for post-baby-boomer set. For them this is not really a family country club; it is a party club. For most of the owners it is a family club, and there is the conflict. This is just a symptom of how out of control it is. If you do not force a change, nothing will change. I wish you luck and will help in any way I can," he said. Donald then got up and left Brad's office.

Brad returned to the pile of incident reports that Donald had compiled from the Gatehouse. On the top was a list of seven missing autos that probably were taken right out of the owners's driveways. Next up was a list of homes that had missing jewelry, and the police had not identified any suspects. The fourth list was a compilation of cars and other vehicles that were believed to be speeding through the community and others that had been seen running stop signs. Finally, a list had been compiled of the owners that had engaged in outrageous behavior at the Pool Bar area. The report detailed incident after incident of excessive drinking, disrespect to any server that suggested they had had enough to drink; another, while intoxicated, had placed a twenty-dollar bill in the bottom of a young woman's bikini swimsuit. Another boasted that he tipped the servers so much that they either loved him or would shield him from management if he was accused of misbehaving at the Pool Bar. Follow-up reports confirmed that this owner was the single largest spender at the Pool Bar during the months of the high season. Clearly, the whole team at the Pool Bar was compromised, and they either could not or would not cut off excessive drinkers.

Brad was overwhelmed by the information he had seen in just his first few hours of his review. He would need to talk to some of the people that had submitted the information that had been compiled in these reports. He asked Janey to get contact information for the complaining owners so he could follow-up with them. He believed some of the reports would not be substantiated, would be incomplete, or would not be confirmed by the persons making the report. Others would not want to take it any further if they had to openly accuse another neighbor of improper conduct. But the information had to be followed up, and it was probably best if he did it as part of his consulting assignment. It would just take some time.

CHAPTER ELEVEN
Jake: Gaming-Learned Strategy

Not only had she disappeared, but Charlie was gone too, and he had to track them down. It had only been a few days, but he had all the tools he needed to locate them. He just had to do it with a little finesse. He did not know what he would do if he found them, but there was no point in leaving a breadcrumb trail as he searched. He went into the storage closet and retrieved a computer that he had claimed from surplus equipment at his firm. He had refurbished it and updated it with a new hard drive. He purchased a burner smartphone for cash that was equally untraceable and capable of linking him to the internet. He entered Alison's Postbook account and found picture after picture of her having the time of her life at a party that looked like it was in a local setting. She had taken a selfie of her and a middle-aged man standing near a pool. This was last night. The guy looked familiar, a rich guy with movie star hair. He entered into another site, the Morning News Briefing, and went through the recent issues. There. His name was Victor Vance, a wealthy mogul that was running a rental company catering to those interested in an active lifestyle. He did some further research and found he had recently closed on a house in a new development called Palm Tree Reserve. It was being built next to the highly successful RP Community. A click onto ICearth and there was an overhead view of the house and all the logical approaches one could take to break into the house. It was amazing what you could see in near real-time. There was no privacy anymore. He could see what flowers were planted around the house, whether the owner had left the hose on in the front yard to water the plants, the kind of car he owned, a Porsche convertible by the way, whether there were any posted security protection signs in the front yard, and whether the road in front of the house was completely paved. Then he turned to tracing Charlie and Alison.

He knew she was actively posting pictures last night so she had another smart phone she must have bought and could be tracked. Charlie had his entry-level game boy with him. Last night they both had been in a house that was located on Martini Drive in the RP Community. But they were not there now. Using ICearth, he spotted her red convertible parked next to Vic's Porsche in Vic's driveway. They were at Vic's house. How could she leave him for that slimy piece of crap? Even if it was a short-term thing, how could she? Just to find a little excitement? How could she take Charlie from him? He was deeply disturbed. This was worse than a divorce. She had walked out on him for some sexual fling. She had not even tried to work things out. This had to end, and if he planned it right, it would, without breadcrumbs.

He went back to ICearth. He could see that driving into the Palm Tree Reserve would be problematic. His research indicated that there were security cameras that protected the main and side entrances to the community and when completed would cover all the homes. But he noted that the fence line between RP and Palm Tree had been taken down during construction and certainly, he thought, without any security cameras at this point. Approaching the house undetected would be easy compared with driving to and from without a trace. He thought about it. The garage beneath the condo tracked every entry and exit of all cars parked there. So that was the first problem. Even if he could avoid the cameras, his car had navigation, and he felt certain sometimes that someone would use the system to track his car's movement. This would require some thought.

CHAPTER TWELVE

Follow-Up: Where Are The Cars

It was important, Brad felt, to understand how a community could have so many missing cars in such a short period of time. Also the number of homes that had jewelry thefts was troubling. Could all of this be related? Were the dates of the car thefts and the burglaries the same? Were the homes near to each other, or were there other patterns? Had non-residents entered the premises from the gates on the nights the thefts occurred? After talking with two of the owners about the jewelry thefts, he found a common thread. Nothing else had been taken according to Susan Doyle, one of the owners who was a victim of a jewelry theft. There was no sign of a breakin. The hiding place, Susan indicated, was not really a hiding place at all. It was the top-right drawer of her bedroom dresser. Susan, a native of Door County, said that is where she always put her jewelry when in Wisconsin. Linda Spicer, originally from St. Louis, kept hers in an empty running-shoe box on a shelf in her bedroom closet. Christy George, who with her husband Lou moved to RP from Cedar Rapids, Iowa, said her jewelry was in a sock under a few stuffed teddy bears in a basket in the corner of the room. Each had admitted that just like their homes up North, they did not lock their front doors at night. The had felt secure that they were well protected by the fence line around their gated community. Because they were each embarrassed by their loss, they had not reported the matter to the police, and it was only after they made a claim to their insurance company that any police were notified. It was only a month later that security found out and that was because the police had contacted the security director. No alerts had been sent out to the Community about the thefts.

Brad asked each of these three women who had recently been in their house before the burglaries. After ticking off the names of neighbors and a few relatives, Brad found out that they had all used the same carpet cleaning firm. None had mentioned this to the police because they all knew the owner of the cleaning company and knew him to be honest. But he had a lot of employees they did not know as well. Brad felt certain that the same firm had several of the other burglarized homes on their customer list. A call to the owner of the cleaning firm confirmed Brad's suspicions. He identified a few new hires that might have been involved. He wanted to help make this right for his customers. Brad said he would note that. He planned to contact the police and give them the information. But he knew that if the Club had collected this information, most of the burglaries could have been prevented. That would particularly be the case if the Club had alerted the owners of reported burglaries and advised all to make sure their homes were locked and valuables secured. That would be in his report for sure.

Next, he would tackle the car thefts. He quickly learned three things. First, the cars could only leave through one of two gates at night: the front gate, right under the nose of the front gate custodian or the rear gate. Second, all the thefts had occurred in perimeter houses that had garages but that every one of the cars were parked outside in their driveways. Third, unless the thefts were perpetrated by someone inside the community, the thief either climbed the fence or rode into the community as a passenger through the front gate. Checking the gate log, there were no car entries by nonresidents on any night the cars were stolen. Could a ring of thefts be engineered by one of the owners or their teenaged children? Possible but not likely, he reasoned. The practical problem with an inside job was that the thief had to get back inside the gate after the theft. That meant two siblings had to be involved or even a parent to drive the thief back into the community. Since several of the thefts happened the same night, that meant a lot of family time in the car. So the probability was that it was a fence climber or two.

He called in Rodrigo Gomez, the facilities manager, and asked a couple of questions about video cameras. Brad had learned that his parents had fled to the US and raised a family while picking vegetables in the Immokalee area. Rodrigo was born in Florida and escaped the subsistence life that his parents had made for themselves as farm workers by studying engineering and graduating college from University of the Gulf. Brad was interested in whether the video capture feature of the cameras was taking pictures of the drivers exiting the gates. Rodrigo, he preferred "Rod," said, "No, it only captures the license plate and records time of exit." He told Brad that other cameras were not operational along the fence line and some of the main streets in RP.

"How long do the videos and pictures get retained?" asked Brad. Rod said only about 24 hours, and it is recorded over the next day. Brad said nothing and then thanked Rod for his information.

Brad contacted about half of the owners whose cars had been stolen. The police had found out nothing. After he spent a little time on the phone with these owners, they admitted that they probably left their cars unlocked and maybe with the keys in them. They were so used to parking the cars in the garage at night that they rarely locked them. Also with all the gizmos in these new cars, most had no real key to insert in the ignition. Usually the key was in the cupholder they said. Brad doubted that information was in the police report or the insurance claim file.

So Brad was pretty sure that the thief just jumped the fence at night, found a home near the fence line with a fancy new car parked in the driveway, opened it, started it, and drove out either gate. It could be one or more people involved, but one mystery was how several cars could be taken in a night if the thief had to walk through the neighborhood, which was quite large. It could be a mile and a half from one stolen car to the second. Maybe many fence jumpers were involved or something else. Maybe they found one car first and drove through the community until they found another. That was a risky strategy since these cars were upscale and probably known to belong to certain owners. He called in Donald and briefed him on his conclusions. Donald's eyes lit up and he suggested that a few of his guys with communication devices plant themselves around the community that night and catch the son-of-a-bitch that was boosting RP cars. Brad said he would tag along, but Donald was in charge. "Make sure we do not leak this to any of the owners, or we could have a vigilante group out in force," Brad said.

Friday night was a prime night for car thefts in the Community. The Pool Bar was serving the usual two drinks for the price of one, and most of the owners who frequented there were home tucked away by eleven P.M. It was a rare owner that made it through the eleven P.M. news. As Donald's team began setting up, they saw that nearly half of the owners of the houses had a car parked in the driveway. The setup for the team was four staff that usually took care of the gatehouse throughout the day and one car that was parked in a parking lot near one of the condo buildings. A little overtime and a hunt for bad guys made recruiting easy for Donald. All were in radio or phone contact. Brad thought that a bicycle might be a good thing to have instead of either sitting in a car or crawling around behind shrubbery or a palm tree. And he could get a bike ride in the next morning. That was the trouble with Tri guys, always thinking about getting in a workout. The neighboring Trek store was willing to rent him a high-end bicycle for a week as long as he agreed to wear a helmet at all times. "Not a problem, Steve," he told the salesman. "I always wear one and brought it with me on the airplane." Steve mounted Brad's special pedals on the bike. They allowed him to clip onto the pedals with his bike shoes. But Brad knew that he would wear his running shoes that night in case he had to chase someone down. It was impossible to run in cleated bike shoes. The team set up around eleven-thirty P.M. and hoped that the thief would appear. Brad sat on his bike in a condo parking lot checking out the closest fence line. Then he saw some movement as something appeared to be thrown over the fence. and landed on the grass. Then another object came sailing over a hedge that blocked a clear view of the fence behind it. Then two figures climbed over the fence, both clothed in black with head covers. Brad blinked, and as the figures picked up the objects that had flown over the fence, he could clearly see what they were. Brad hit his head with his hand. They were mountain bikes! Two mountain bikes! No wonder they could speed around the Community so quickly, case out multiple cars, and get away so quickly. The bikes were compact enough that they could easily fit into the trunk of a sedan or the back of an SUV. Brilliant! They could cruise silently through the neighborhood, stopping at just the car they wanted to steal. If spotted, they could move on quickly to the next car. He called Donald and relayed what he had seen. Donald contacted the Fort Myers police detectives that had been investigating the car thefts, and they came running. The biking duo quickly moved in on their prey. A BMW hardtop convertible was checked out and passed their muster, unlocked, and the key was in the coffee holder. The next driveway had a Porsche SUV which also met their standards for theft. Almost choreographed like a ballet dance, the bikes were loaded into the trunks of the cars, already running. They quietly pulled out of the driveways and sped toward the front gate. Donald had positioned his guys so they could photograph and video the cars as they went through the Community. Then as they exited though the front gate, the guard on duty took a video of the cars exiting and of the police vehicles pulling them over as they attempted to enter the highway outside RP. It was a glorious sight! The police forced them out of the cars, cuffed them. and underneath their hoods, they found two young men, barely out of high school. The exit was marked with crime scene tape and was surrounded by cop cars, all flashing their red, blue and white lights. Donald introduced Brad to Detective Wilbur Cross who was in charge of the major crimes section of the police department. Eventually, the arrest of these two young felons led to a highly organized car theft ring and associated chop shop. A few fly-by-night used car dealers were involved. The crime statistics for all of Fort Myers improved as the ring was routinely hitting 10 other communities in the city and county.

The report was writing itself, thought Brad. Keep your cars garaged, lock your vehicles at night, don't leave valuables in the car at night, and don't leave your keys in the car. Video capture of all vehicles coming and going through the front and back gates is essential. No-one could drive through the fence line given the hedges, shrubbery, and ponds near the fences. But when you used video, it was just as important to capture the face of the driver as it was to take a picture of the licenses. That would all be in the report, he thought, as a recommendation. While the night ended early for Brad and Donald's security guys, other things were afoot in the dark at RP.

Chapter Thirteen

In The Middle Of The Night:

Stealth Visit To River Palms

Jake had spent the day thinking how to get to the luxury home in Palm Tree Reserve owned by Vic Vance. His visit to the ICearth website confirmed Alison's car was parked there in the driveway. He looked at the aerial view of the adjoining RP community and noted that the fence line between RP and the construction project at Palm Tree was almost nonexistent. But there was more. One of the borders of RP was the river that flowed by the property and continued on to the Gulf. The current was not very swift, and paddle crafts had no problem moving up and down the river. The year before he had enrolled in the University of the Gulf night school, Alison had purchased an inflatable one-person kayak from Amazon as a surprise. Before he had even opened the Amazon packaging, he was starting night classes. He had simply put the box in the storage unit assigned to his condo unit and forgotten about it until now. He got the box, brought it back to his condo, and opened it. It came with a lightweight backpack, and he read the instructions. He was surprised at how light the kayak was. It was less than 10 pounds, including the portable pump and collapsible paddle. He could easily carry the uninflated kayak from his condo to the headwater of the river, paddle down the river, and under cover of darkness, enter the RP property at the boat ramp located in the boat recreation area of RP. If he could avoid the security cameras near his parking garage, he could easily walk a mile carrying the backpack, quickly pump up the kayak, and launch it. He could walk across the RP property and to the Palm Tree Reserve and to Vic's house. It looked to be about a half mile from the boat ramp to Vic's. The only drawback was the yellow trim around the top of the kayak. Well, it was dark, and it would be night; who would see?

What he would do when he got to Vic's he had not definitely decided, but he had solved the problem of getting there and back without a car. But first he needed to practice. He wanted to be able to inflate the kayak with his eyes closed, mimicking the darkness. It was just as important to repack it after he got back to his launch point. After the third try, he felt he got it. He deflated it, packed it along with the paddle and pump in the backpack and turned to his apparel for the trip. He picked through his closet and found a long sleeve black shirt and dark pants and black running shoes, making sure that there were no day glow tags on anything. He was satisfied with his outfit and dressed. He went back to the computer and identified the best landing point at RP and the best route through RP to the back fence. He had hacked into the security system of both RP and Palm Tree and found there were few if any video cameras within the Community, but he could not count out these doorbell cameras that owners may have installed. So he planned a route that would keep him in the shadows. That would be the best he could do. He erased all data on the hard drive, disconnected the computer, pulled the hard drive, and placed the computer shell back into the storage space. He wiped all fingerprints from the hard drive and placed it in the backpack. He planned to dump it somewhere in the river. His gaming helped with the planning, but what would he really do when he got there? Could he get Alison to come back to him? Could he really hurt someone? Would it really make Alison come back to him? Maybe he would have to force things. He thought even if he could not make her come back, he could at least beat the crap out of Vic. There would be a sense of satisfaction in that. He could not bring a Louisville Slugger bat with him, but he had just what he needed: a metal, expandable baton used by law enforcement in riots or crowd control. He had picked it up at a gun show earlier that day and had paid cash for it. He thought it was untraceable. But it might not be enough. Maybe he would need a gun. He found the handgun that Alison had urged him to buy for her in a private sale once she became pregnant with Charlie. She wanted the feeling of security when Jake was not around. She was always comfortable with guns and kept it clean, lubricated, and locked away. He found the key, unlocked it, made sure it was loaded, and decided to bring it as well. He packed both the baton and the gun in the backpack.

Just before midnight Friday, he left his condo and walked down the back stairs, carefully avoiding the security cameras that were aimed at the main entrance to the building. He held the backpack like a sack of trash just in case and walked back towards the dumpsters and disappeared into the wooded area behind his condo. It led to a boat ramp. This was an important amenity of his condo complex and would be where he could launch his kayak. Fifteen minutes later he packed everything he needed into the inflated kayak and began paddling the two mile stretch down to the RP boat dock. Shortly after he launched, he dumped the hard drive in the middle of the river.

It took less than an hour of slow paddling to reach the RP boat dock. He went around it to the sand beach and landed the kayak and pulled it into the tree line. He used the same backpack that held the kayak, placed a few items in it, and set off across the RP property keeping to the shadows. He could see where a fence had been planned along all the riverbank except where the dock and beach were. Fortunately, most of the route he had laid out in his mind cut right through the golf course. It was as quiet as a cemetery. Earlier, as he was paddling down the river, he had noticed a lot of police activity near the entrance to RP, but that had disappeared by the time he had arrived. But it made him even more cautious. He knew from the aerial photos that the golf course was full of ponds that the golfers dreaded but were an integral part of the community's storm water system that fed into the river. Caution was dictated in the dark now and when he returned.

He knew what house he was looking for. It was just as ICearth had shown. Alison's car was in the driveway, its new car shine seemingly mocking him. What was he thinking when he leased it for her, that she would love him more? And what was she thinking hanging out with this sleazy mogul? He noted that there were no operating streetlights near Vic's house. The street was yet to be paved, so it was difficult to walk across the street without a sound, the gravel rocks clicking as he stepped. He moved to the back of the darkened house. He stopped and viewed the pool and patio. This was no plunge pool. It was a full-sized resort pool designed for lap swimming, and the patio must have had twenty lounge chairs around on the deck. Look at all this wealth. It made him sick to look. Focus, focus, he thought. He reached into his backpack and pulled out a screwdriver to jimmy the back slider but was surprised to find it was unlocked and easily slid open. He went inside. No motion sensitive lights. No alarm. Everything was quiet. While it was dark in the house, he had enough visibility to find the staircase. The developer's design for this home had shown two large bedrooms at the top of the stairs and a walkway to two other smaller bedrooms. When he reached the top of the stairs, he again reached into the backpack and felt for the handgun in the bottom. It felt cool even with the driving gloves he had put on before he had entered the house. The gun was untraceable. At least there was no record of his ownership. Would the previous owner remember him? He could not rule that out. But could he really shoot anyone? Would he? Having a gun was one thing; executing someone was another. He pulled it out and stood at the top of the stairs thinking a moment. There was a designer table in the hallway between the rooms. As he was thinking, he slowed his breathing down a bit and realized he could smell Alison's favorite perfume. He followed his nose toward the bedroom on the right. The jasmine scent was confirmed as he saw Alison sleeping with Charlie in the bed with her. He took in her scent and quietly turned away. He could not harm Alison. Vic must be across the hall. Jake went back to the head of the stairs and paused. It was decision time. Maybe he should just beat the crap out of Vic and let it go at that. He was mad at what Alison had done to him. Maybe he could scare Vic a little, and she would come back to him. He put the handgun down on the table and again reached into the backpack and pulled out a steel baton that expanded to three feet. He flicked it and it easily expanded to its full length without a sound. He stepped into Vic's room and moved toward the bed, reached back to swing the baton at Vic and then everything went side-ways. He remembered swinging and hitting Vic, getting caught up in the infernal bedspread, seeing a gun and swinging the baton again, hitting something, and then there were two gunshots as he fell to the floor. He closed his eyes and waited until the smoke cleared.

Minutes later he picked himself off the floor. He looked at the bed and saw Vic, quite dead. He moved to the hallway and saw Alison lying on the floor holding the gun he had bought for her protection in her hand. Her eyes were open, looking at him. Her face was lifeless. He checked her pulse. She was not coming back to him. "What can I do," he thought, "but get out of here?" Surely someone must have heard the shots. He panicked and fled the house. He was not sure what had happened, but it was too late to do anything now. He had to get out of there. He ran back to the dilapidated fence separating Palm Tree from RP and slowed to a walk. He returned to the beach where he had left the kayak, dragged it to the water and then climbed in. He was back at the original launch site, deflated the boat and repacked it in the backpack and went back to the condo. He tried to sleep but nothing came. What had happened? How could he have left Alison in a heap at the top of the stairs? How could he have left Charlie? How will Charlie ever unsee Alison's lifeless body? What kind of father was he?

Chapter Fourteen

Alison: Excitement Ends

Alison, after spending an exciting evening at the Party House the previous night, awoke Friday morning to the smell of coffee, got out of the big bed in the master bedroom, and went downstairs to the kitchen. She found Kaleisha and Charlie sitting and having breakfast. She gave Charlie a hug, and he gave her a big kiss and told her how his room was filled with stuffed animals and toy cars and trucks. Kaleisha said he had been up for two hours playing. She was not sure he really wanted to come down for breakfast, but she had to have her coffee. But Charlie must have been really hungry as he ate two big pancakes and a bowl of fruit loops. Alison poured herself a cup of coffee and sat down. Kaleisha asked if pancakes were OK, and Alison said they were fine. She asked where Vic was and Kaleisha said he had gone into the office for an hour or so and that he would be back in time to prepare for tonight's party. The guests would be arriving at six P.M. She said that Vic had booked another member into the Master Suite at the Party House but that Alison could either move to another room in the Party House or move her things to Vic's house in Palm Tree Reserve. Kaleisha said, "If you look out the window of the master bedroom here, you can see his house. You and Charlie could move in this morning. The pool is heated and there is food in the pantry." Kaleisha said, "I will come by this afternoon and watch Charlie so you can go to the party tonight." Alison said she would like to go to Vic's place and packed her and Charlie's bags. She followed Kaleisha's directions and was soon parked in Vic's driveway. This house was even grander than the Party House. She and Charlie changed into their bathing suits and jumped into the pool. It was large enough to swim laps. It also had a section that was shallow enough for Charlie to walk in without the water going over his waist. She checked out the pantry and the fridge and made some lunch for Charlie and herself but concluded that she would call El Nino's for a pizza for Charlie for dinner. When Maria answered the phone, Alison had to tell her that the delivery was to the Vance residence in Palm Tree Reserve and not to her old condo. Maria paused when she got that information and said, "Got it, delivery at 5:45 at 201 Palm Tree Way in Palm Tree Reserve and bill to your account." Charlie took a nap while Alison started getting ready for the party and her hostess duties. The bath was great, particularly after she found the controls for the Jacuzzi settings. She had not felt so relaxed in months. She thought about the night with Vic. The whole night was an exciting adventure, but on the whole Jack was a better lover than Vic. Vic was a better catch. For one thing he was fabulously wealthy, measured by all the possessions he had: his Porsche convertible, his house, his business, and rich friends. Jake was not. Jake was Jake: plain old, boring Jake. But Jake was Charlie's father and did provide well for them. Was that enough? As she got ready, she applied a few drops of her favorite perfume. Jake had ordered it for her. He was always doing things like that.

Vic drove into the driveway of his house around three P.M. and went upstairs and found Alison sitting at the dressing table and said, "Hello my love, do we have time before we go to the party for a little fun?"

She looked at his reflection in the dressing room mirror, put all thoughts of Jake out of her mind, and said, "Of course. I have been waiting all day for you."

They came up for air around five P.M. and Alison showered quickly and then dressed for the evening. Vic took his time watching Alison shower, dry herself off, dress, and put on her makeup. She watched him again in the mirror and could see that he was aroused again just watching her. Finally, he went into the shower, and then she heard the doorbell and dashed downstairs. It was the delivery guy from El Nino's. Charlie and Kaleisha were already taking the pizza box from him when Alison moved around them and signed for the delivery and gave him a good gratuity.

They hopped into Vic's convertible and drove over to the Party House and were there to greet the first wave of guests. He took his time, not wanting to muss either Alison's hair or his. A seemingly endless line of limos stood in the culdesac waiting to unload the men and women guests eager to party. The music was blaring, but it was not as loud as Thursday night. When she mentioned this to Vic, he pointed out a few older men across the room. He said they were members of the board of RP and said, "They had asked that the noise level be lower tonight." She nodded and then noticed that they were all either drinking the free booze or dancing with some of the young women.

She looked at Vic and said, "As long as they are happy, right?"

"You got that right," he laughed.

Around eleven P.M., Alison said, "I want to go and check on Charlie. He has not been away from home two nights in a row. I know that Kaleisha is taking good care of him, but he needs his mother."

Vic signaled to one of his assistants, Ashley, and asked her to take over because he and Alison were leaving. He said, "You can reach me on my cell if anything comes up."

As Vic got into the car, Alison said, "Thank you, Vic. I understand if you have to get back and take care of the business. There are just sometimes a mother has to do things."

Vic leaned over and kissed her and started the car. He said, "The party is in good hands with Ashley, and we have the night to ourselves if Charlie is adjusting OK."

Alison checked in on Charlie who was sleeping in the guest bedroom across the hallway from the master bedroom. He was at peace. She could hear his breathing as she stood over him. He was wearing his favorite pajamas, which were decorated with giraffes. She pulled up the covers and left the room.

Alison went into the master bedroom and said, "Vic, I think

there are a few positions that we have not tried yet." Vic, at first was surprised at her words and then smiled, got up from the bed and embraced her. As midnight approached, they were exhausted, and Alison gave Vic a goodnight kiss, gathered her clothes, and went into the guest room. She spent some time in the adjoining bathroom, put on her pajamas, and climbed into bed with Charlie. Alison had left her door open and could hear Vic snoring loudly from the master bedroom. She closed her eyes and fell into a light sleep, still hearing the snoring and dreaming of the events of the last two days and holding Charlie close to her. But Alison sensed something. It was a breathing different than Charlie's or the snoring from the other room. It seemed like someone was in the room, but when she opened up her eyes, no one was there. She closed her eyes and rolled back over to Charlie's side of the bed. But sleep would not come. Something was not right. She quietly got out of bed, slipped on a robe, and crept into the hall. She looked around in the darkness of the hallway and noticed a handgun on the hall table. That had not been there when she went to bed. It was the same caliber as the one Jake had bought for her. She paused and picked it up. She had grown up with weapons in her parent's house and was a proficient shot. The gun felt good in her hand, just like hers. She moved towards Vic's room, the gun held down by her thigh. She heard a shout in Vic's room and rushed in, saw two figures in the room, both male and leaning over the bed. One had already swung an object through the air and was striking again when she fired. From the bed another shot rang out. She collapsed on the floor. This was not good. It hurt so bad, she thought, as she descended into darkness. The party was over.

CHAPTER FIFTEEN

Brad: Dogs

Brad got back Saturday morning from his quick run, took his shower, and stepped into the kitchen. Kate gave him a cup of coffee, and they talked while sitting at the kitchen counter. She pointed at the flatscreen tv and the morning news. NBC2 was reporting on a double killing at the Palm Tree Reserve last night. She said that was the development next door to RP. Other than reporting on the deaths, there was no further information provided by the news station. He asked Kate what she was going to do today. She thought she would check out some houses in the area to get decorating ideas, she said. "I planned to have lunch with Robin. She wanted to show me her new landscaping project, and I want to show her the golf outfits I bought."

"Sure," he said. "But I would not go anywhere close to the Palm Tree Reserve. It is not only too expensive, but it will be crawling with police." He kissed her goodbye and went into the office. He placed a call to Detective Cross's office. He was the chief of major crimes and in charge of the investigation of the car thefts at RP. Brad wanted to know if there was any more information that was needed to prosecute them. He was told by an officer that he was out of the office working the double killing, information they probably should not have shared. He thanked the officer and left a message. He spent a few moments on the Fort Myers website and learned a few things about Cross. He was born in Biloxi, Mississippi, to sharecropper parents. He probably would have never gotten beyond the barriers to a black youth in the south but for his athletic prowess. It did not matter that he was class valedictorian of his high school class, it was football that got him a scholarship into college. That is where the name rang a bell. Wilbur Cross, star linebacker for FSU and a cup of coffee with the Philadelphia Eagles and now chief detective in the Fort Myers police department. Interesting. He returned to the stack of reports.

The next report on the list was the party atmosphere at the Pool Bar and at some of the rental homes. He was paging through the complaints when Janey knocked on the door of the office and said, "Duke asked that you see Mrs. Lynn Dorfman who is in the foyer of the Clubhouse."

"Any idea what it is about?" he asked.

Janey said, "Well she usually complains about the dogs in the community. Owners do not pick up after the dogs; some owners refuse to use a leash, and a few have bitten people walking while the dogs roamed unleashed. She did not say what was troubling her."

"Bring her back." he said. Janey brought her back and introduced them. "Hello Mrs. Dorfman. How can I help you? I am Brad Pope, helping out here for a few days. Janey mentioned your interest in dogs in the Community," he said.

"I love dogs. I have one myself and I keep it under control, and I pick up after her. But this is not about dogs. It's about what I saw last night," she said.

"Please sit down and tell me what is on your mind," he said. She had a lot to say.

Before she began, Brad asked her what kind of dog she had. "Baby is a Westie," she said.

He said, "I have noticed about a dozen of that type around the Community while on my run, and I wondered if it was one dog that was being walked by multiple people or if I was seeing things."

She laughed, "No, once I got my Baby everyone in my bridge group wanted one just like it, and you are right; there are twelve all from the same breeder. Anyway, I wanted to let someone know what Baby and I saw last night. Baby is getting on in years now, and I have to walk her in a baby stroller when she needs to go out to pee. Lately, she has been waking me up in the middle of the night to go out, and I have not been getting much sleep. Last night around midnight, after all that commotion with the car thieves and the police, Baby wanted to go out. So I got the baby stroller from the garage. We have to store it out there now because Baby sometimes does not let us know soon enough when she needs to get out to pee, and well, it's better to let it dry out in the garage than inside. We must have gotten out to the sidewalk around twelve-fifteen A.M. when I see a dark figure walking right in the middle of the golf course. Looked to me like the person was wearing very dark clothes. But Baby yipped to get out of the stroller and then my attention was focused on making sure that if Baby left a mess, I could clean it up. Can't call out people for not picking up after their dogs if you don't do it yourself." Brad laughed at that and asked if that was all she saw. "No," she said. "About thirty minutes after we got back from the walk, Baby began to whine again. I spent some time talking to her just to make sure that she really had to go this soon. You know now why I am not getting much sleep. So back out we went. We were almost in the same place when I looked up and saw what must have been the same dark figure on the golf course but this time walking the opposite way and moving very quickly. Not exactly running but, you know, maybe jogging. Before Baby started whining to get out, I must have stared for a good two minutes, and I think I know where the person was going."

Brad paused and asked, "Where do you think this person was going? Do you think it was one of the car thieves that got away?"

"No, this person was headed for the boat area, but I suppose that it could have been one of your thieves making a getaway. After Baby finished with her second pee, we went back inside. All I know is that the only time I have ever seen someone on the golf course that late was Diane Proust's husband sneaking back drunk from one of those party events. This was different. The same person walking back and forth in the middle of the night. It made me so worried, I could not get back to sleep. So here I am."

Brad had a few more questions, but Lynn was pretty sure this was the same person both times. He asked her if she would mind showing him the location of the sighting. She said she really would like to have him come out and see for himself. Lynn said she had driven a golf cart to the Clubhouse, and if he followed her, she would lead the way. He arranged a cart through Janey and followed Lynn through the Community. Once they reached the Dorfman's house and she stopped to point out the location of her sighting, it was clear that she had to be right. There were no houses or condos in the direction the person was heading last night. The only logical end point was the boat area. Brad thanked Lynn and drove his cart down the street to the boat area and stopped. As Duke had explained to him on the grand tour, the boat area consisted of a small rectangular boat house that stored several canoes, life jackets, paddles, several paddle boards and kayaks, and rescue gear in case a boater got into trouble within reach of the boat manager on duty. There of course was a dock that was used for offloading small motorized crafts with a shallow draft. The river was not particularly deep but could handle shallow draft boats. The beach was next to the boat dock and was ideal for supervised play of owners and guests and the launching and beaching of canoes, paddle boards, and kayaks. But this was a natural river and creatures lived in it and along the banks. Snakes, otter, river rats, and the occasional alligator were not uncommon, so there was great emphasis on adult supervision and vigilance. The signage was conspicuous and clear. Brad got out of the cart to look around. The boat house was locked, and there were no signs anyone had gotten in or tried to. When the boat house opened around ten A.M., he would call the aquatics recreation director and have her verify that. He walked to the end of the dock and looked up and down the river. He could see a ways up and down the river but nothing out of the ordinary. As he walked back from the end of the dock, he looked down at the beach on his left and could see drag marks. Some craft had either landed and been dragged over the sand to the trees behind the boathouse or dragged from the trees to the water and launched. It could have been the last boat out Friday afternoon, but he understood that the aquatics recreational director's duties included grooming the sand at the end of the day. He got out his phone and fired off several photos. If you looked closely, you could see depressions in the sand by the drag marks. Those had to be depressions made by the person that Lynn had seen walking on the golf course not 200 yards away from this location. He walked back to the cart and found a legal pad he carried with him while working on his study. He pulled out his pen and wrote, "BOAT AREA CLOSED TEMPORARILY. DO NOT ENTER OR DISTURB ANYTHING." He found a tack on the bulletin board at the boathouse and posted his note, reminding himself to call the aquatics recreation director to arrange a more permanent sign.

He drove the cart back to the Clubhouse. On the way he waved to Lynn Dorfman. Then after making the last turn towards the Clubhouse, he spotted another woman walking her dog in a stroller. He stopped and asked if it would be OK for him to take a photo of the lady, her stroller, and dog. As he drove away, he thought "Kate will get a kick out of this!" Back at the Clubhouse, he called Detective Cross's office again. This time he was put through. He introduced himself as a former Secret Service agent and now consulting at RP on security. Cross remembered him from the arrests the night before of the young punks that were stealing cars from RP residents. Brad reported his conver sations with Mrs. Dorfman and his trip to the boat house and said he would forward the pictures from his phone. Cross said to send what he had and that he would arrange for one of his detectives to check out the boathouse area. Brad called the aquatics recreation director and briefed her about the signage that needed to go up and why the area needed to be secured until the police could release the area for use by the Club. Time for a cup of Joe.

Brad stepped into Duke's office. "Want a cup of coffee?" he asked. "I want to update you on what I have been doing the last few days." Brad then gave him a summary of his findings as to the burglary ring and the car thefts.

Duke sat there with his mouth open, stunned. "You mean that we caught the car thieves in the act?" he asked.

"Yes, of course there may be more involved, like body shops or secondhand car dealers or cross state buyers or even internet rings that seek out specific cars to steal, like that movie that Nicolas Cage was in. We did our part and will let the police handle the rest. But we might have additional information the police may want to examine. While it may be unrelated to the car thefts, we think that someone was trespassing through the community last night in addition to the two car thieves. I have alerted Detective Cross, and one of his people will be out to check out the story and look at the evidence. Also the police are closing in on the dry-cleaning firm and have learned that the same couple was on the cleaning crew at every house that was burglarized. We will hear when they are picked up."

"That is just outstanding," Duke said. "I will join you for coffee." Brad called Kate and asked if she was up for picnic at the beach. She said, "It sounds great, but I assume you want me to bring your swim gear."

"How well you know me. I know a great restaurant that is getting rave reviews in North Naples called Cote d'Azur, which has the greatest seafood done in a French style. I also hear their duck entree is really popular. I can have Janey make us a reservation. She knows the owners James and Dar Waller. See you in five."

Chapter Sixteen

Jake: Lose Threads

He spent the night tossing and turning. Maybe he got a few hours of rest, but it was not sleep. She must be dead. He had looked into her lifeless eyes before he left the house. What the hell had happened? He knew his gun was missing. Had Alison found it? How many shots had been fired? Did not figure this guy Vic had a gun, but he was waving something around when he tripped in the bedding. He remembers hitting Vic with the baton but not where he had aimed. Alison, dead! If he had not gone to the house last night, she would be alive. That guy Vic certainly looked dead when he checked him. Both dead. He just wanted Alison home. Check the news, he thought. There might be something on NBC2 by now. He turned it on, and the newscaster was describing what had been reported. Two bodies had been found at a house in Palm Tree Reserve, a male and female. No names were disclosed. The newscaster said that the house belonged to a Victor Vance who was believed to be in residence. The media were awaiting further information from the police. A press briefing was scheduled for later in the day. Jake knew that the police would be coming soon. It was just a question of time. Keep it together.

The doorbell rang at ten A.M. on Saturday. Jake went downstairs and opened the door. There he saw several law enforcement folks. Before he could ask them why they were there, the woman directly in front asked him if his name was Jake Reynolds. "Yes, what is this about?" he asked calmly.

"Mr. Reynolds, I am Officer Zendaya Budd, and I regret to inform you that your wife was shot and killed last night at a residence in Palm Tree Reserve. Your son Charlie was found in the residence and is in the custody of child protective services," she said. "Do you know any reason why she would have been in Palm Tree with your son?"

He stood there in shock, his shoulders just dropping as he seemed to lose his balance. His voice quivering, he said, "We have been having marriage difficulties, and she left a message that she was taking Charlie and going away for the weekend. I have not seen them since Thursday morning. Alison is dead? How did it happen?"

Officer Budd said, "The matter is under investigation."

"How can I get Charlie back? He needs his Dad," Jake said.

Here is the number for DCPS," said officer Budd, adding, "Can we come in and ask you a few questions. This is detective George who is working on the investigation."

He said, "Yes, come in. I don't know if I am up to this. This is just unbelievable! Alison dead! I want to help in any way I can, but my first priority is making sure that Charlie is safe and home as soon as possible." He asked how it had happened.

"What can you tell me?" detective George asked. Jake said that he had gotten her message but had no idea where she went. He thought of tracking her phone, but something was wrong because he found her phone in the bedroom. He had been unable to contact her since Thursday. He said that since she said she would be gone for the weekend, he decided to wait until she came back or contacted him. Detective George and Officer Budd stayed an hour, peppering him with questions about where he was last evening and where he thought his wife was going and asking for the text message that Alison had left. He showed them his phone and gave them Alison's as well. They asked if he could come this afternoon and confirm the identity of Alison but that it was a formality. The police were certain that the woman they had found was Alison.

After the police left, he sat in the living room thinking. He had done his best to be a grieving husband and a concerned Dad. But he knew he had not convinced either of them. He just hoped that he had not left a trail. He had not killed her. But, damn it, he was there, and she was gone. They did not tell him anything about that guy Vic. Only the news caster said anything about Vic. Chapter Seventeen

CHAPTER SEVENTEEN
Detective Cross:
The Investigation

Cross had Officer Budd and Detective George in his office after their return from Jake's place. Budd had been the officer that had responded to the call from the Vance house, and George thought it might be helpful if she could accompany him to Jake's house. She had grown up in Fort Myers being raised in the Harlem Heights section of town. Zendaya had a good rapport with people and was a good investigator. George thought it would lower Jake's guard if she gave him the news and helped with the interview. They summarized what they had learned. Zendaya summarized the interview with Jake: "Basically, Alison and Jake were getting divorced but still living together with their son Charlie. Alison told him she was going away for the weekend and took Charlie with her."

George picked up the findings so far: "So she goes to a party and hooks up with this guy, Victor Vance, and goes to his house. We don't know enough about why or how she found out about this party, but we have her computer and phone and are having the contents reviewed by our technicians. Alison was with Victor in his house last night. It looks like he was in one room, and she and her son were in another when, sometime after midnight, they shot each other. Each was found with a gun in their possession. Each gun was fired. Forensics will tell us which bullets came from which gun and any other evidence that can be found on the guns, such as fingerprints and gunshot residue. But preliminarily, it is pretty clear that each fired a gun last night. The kid was sleeping at the time and heard the gun shots, got up, and went to the caretaker's room to see if his mother was there. The caretaker, Kaleisha Campbell, a Jamaican-American, had heard the shots, and when Charlie found her, she was up and out of bed. She made him wait in her room as she went to Victor's room and found both bodies. She was certain they were dead but called 911 to ask for police and an ambulance for both. She said she heard nothing before the gunshots. Didn't see anyone else. Has no idea why they would have shot each other as they had retired to Vic's bedroom after returning from a party. She also told us that she had brought Alison's and Charlie's things up to the bedroom and had unpacked their suitcases. Did not see any weapon in her bags. Kaleisha did say that she had no idea whether Alison carried a gun in her purse or had one in her car."

Detective Cross said, "Put the reports together and file them." He asked George to go out to RP and find out if there was anything to the golf course story. "And get all the information on these guns. Did Vance own one, did Alison own one, and if not, where she got it. But from everything you have found out so far, it was just a shootout, and they killed one another." He called down to the public affairs officer and asked her to come up.

Cross asked Officer Loraine Kraft to release the information on both victims and the apparent shooting of each other and indicate that no motive had been determined. The son was unharmed and was being released to the father. While further investigation would continue, the preliminary findings indicated no one else was involved in the shootings. Cross said, "Let the press know that a press briefing would be held around five-thirty P.M., in time for the evening TV news."

Detective George spent a half hour with Brad and got the information he had from the boathouse area. He told Brad that it just looked to the police like this was a shootout and that there were no other suspects. The boathouse incident was probably a trespasser and not related to anything at all. Brad thanked him for looking into the matter and was walking him to the door when Brad asked if the shooting could have anything to do with the Party House at Martini Drive. "Why do you ask?" asked the detective.

"Well, I checked with our security department and they said this guy Vic was well known in our community. He leased several homes here and used some of those to entertain members of his party club. Limos came into RP and left at all hours carrying these guests to the so called Party House. Incidentally, it is just a stone's throw from the crime scene. Due to the construction at the Palm Tree Reserve, the existing fence line had large segments that were removed. But if no one else is involved it is probably nothing,'" said Brad. "I was just curious. I was just getting into a stack of complaints about the Party House and felt if you had any information about it, it might help me with my review." The detective said that they knew Vance had held parties in various neighborhoods, including RP, but it just looked like a shootout to his chief, Detective Cross. He added that the investigation was, of course, not complete. Detective George was leaving when Brad stopped him with another question.

CHAPTER EIGHTEEN

Detective Cross:

Can We Wrap This Thing Up

Cross had just finished the press briefing when he sat down with Detective George and Officer Budd. Officer Budd reported on what Forensics and the techies reported: "Forensics shows that each victim fired the gun found near their bodies and the bullets fired from each respective gun had struck the other and killed them. The gunshots were not consistent with murder-suicide. The time of each death does not indicate any discernible gap between the other. Victor's gun was registered to him. Alison's handgun was reportedly sold by the owner in a private sale. The interview with the registered owner of record does not support that Alison was the purchaser. It was a white male and perhaps a straw purchase, so that is a loose end. The only operational cameras in the Palm Tree Reserve community are at the front entrance to the community and only show Vance's car entering the community a little after 11 PM."

Detective George jumped in, "I did visit with Brad Pope at RP, and he impressed me. I heard he was retired Secret Service. As I was leaving, he asked me a question: 'Suppose there was someone else there Friday night. How would they get there and leave, knowing that the front entrance of Palm Tree Reserve was monitored by a video security system.' I thought it was worth talking a bit more and he reminded me that this Party House that Vance leases is probably about two hundred yards from Vance's home in Palm Tree Reserve and that there is almost no fence separating the two communities while construction is going on. Brad then went back to his golf course walker and pointed out that someone could have walked from the Vance house through the narrowest part of the RP community to the golf course and exited by the boat house. Or someone from the party at the Party House could have walked over to the Vance house and returned without anyone noticing." Detective George paused a beat and continued, "I asked him whether RP had any security footage that might pick up either situation, but Brad said putting up internal security was under consideration but for now nothing existed with RP's security. But he did say that many of the owners had doorbell security and that some footage might exist." Brad indicated he could have the RP security crew request the video access from nearby owners and if anything came up, he would advise me. Detective George reported, "I told Brad it might be a good idea just to confirm the nonexistence of an unknown third party but not to get too worked up about it. I also asked Brad not to tell any of the RP owners that there was a search for some third party on the loose. Didn't want some social media rumor getting out that we think that this might not be an open and shut case of a shootout."

Cross thanked them both for their update and said he was going home for the evening. As he walked to his car, he began thinking. How had Alison gotten the gun if she did not buy it from the previous owner? And what if the doorbell videos did show a midnight walker near the Party house? How would that be connected with the shooting? Maybe there was something else going on. "I might give Brad a visit before we declare this thing over."

Chapter Nineteen

Jake: Academy Award Performance

Immediately after he learned from the police that Alison was killed, Jake had contacted Alison's parents and informed them of Alison's death and gave them as much information that he had heard from the news media. He said that he was picking up Charlie from DCPS, but if they could manage to come and stay with him, he would really appreciate it. Alison's mother said they would come over that afternoon. Before he went to pick up Charlie, he went to the storage unit and checked on the kayak sitting in the backpack. It was a little wet. He decided he would take it up to the condo and air it out on the porch. The porch got plenty of sun, and it would probably be dry in no time at all. After he carried the backpack to the porch and placed it in the sun, he found the collapsed baton in the bottom of the pack. He had hit Vic once or twice with it. There might be some evidence on the instrument. He could not rule it out. He could not get rid of it now because the police would be back, and going to the river was not too smart. There was a hidden ledge above the storage unit door that would neatly hide the baton. He left it in the pack and carried the pack back down to the storage unit, removed the baton, and placed it on the ledge.

He called Officer Budd and made arrangements to see Alison's body. That was an ordeal. He could barely keep it together. He just kept saying to himself, "I did not shoot her. It's not my fault." The more he thought it, the less convinced he was.

He then went to the offices of the DCPS to pick up Charlie. Charlie was so happy to see his Dad that Jake's eyes teared as Charlie embraced him. The protective services agent did suggest that Jake consider using the counseling services at their offices as losing a mother like that would affect Charlie. Jake said he understood and asked for an appointment with a counselor for Monday, if possible. When he got home Alison's mother was there and picked Charlie up and hugged and kissed him before handing him to Charlie's grandfather for a similar ritual. Charlie seemed to relax. But Jake knew it would just be a while before he started wondering where his mother was. That was going to be a difficult conversation.

As he was thinking about how that conversation would go, his doorbell rang, and a reporter from NBC2 was at the door. She wanted to ask for an on-air interview. Another tv station was there as well and asked if a joint on-camera interview could be conducted. Jake agreed to do it downstairs in front of his condo building in a few minutes.

Jake went downstairs and met NBC2 reporter Ashley Monroe and ABC7 reporter Petrof Manheim who would take his statement and ask questions. Ashley Monroe began her on site broadcast with a short introduction, "I am here with Jake Reynolds, whose wife Alison Reynolds was killed last night at a house in Palm Tree Reserve, is there anything you would like to say Mr. Reynolds?"

Jake looked into the cameras and began with a short statement. "Last night my wife Alison was shot and killed in the house of Victor Vance. My wife and I were going through the early stages of divorce, but we were still seeking ways to reconcile. She told me that she needed some space as we explored our future and went away for the weekend. I do not know Mr. Vance and have no idea when Alison first met him. My son and I and Alison's family are grieving for our loss. I am confident that the police will get to the bottom of all of this. As you can imagine, this is very devastating for all of us. I would prefer to just give you this brief statement and request out of respect for us at this time of deep loss not to answer any questions." He turned away from Ashley, Petrof, and the camera crews and went back inside the condo building. And the Academy Award goes to…

CHAPTER TWENTY

Brad: Ding Dong

As Brad was looking at the five doorbell feeds that he was given access to, he watched Jake's live interview and was impressed. It was well spoken, conveyed a crisp storyline, and said the words of grief and devastation, but, in Brad's opinion, the statement was empty. There was nothing there. Well, it was clear from what Detective George told him, this Jake could not have shot his wife or Victor. But his lack of grief, even if he was reconciled to losing his wife through divorce, was surprising. "Well, let me get this doorbell thing off my mind." Then he clicked on the video from the first house on the north side of the Martini and spotted someone in a dark outfit walking in front of the house. This person, a male, was of average height and seemed to have a pack on his back that was very much lighter than his clothing. He was headed in the direction of the Palm Tree Reserve. About forty-five minutes later, according to the time stamp on the video, the same person, or at least it looked to be the same person, came back in front of the house from the direction of the Palm Tree community. This was more than just a dog walker taking a Westy to pee. This video was something to think about. Maybe not a shooter but something else?

Brad downloaded both clips to his phone and sent them to Detective George and a copy to Officer Budd. He wrote, "You might want to look at these before any of the RP owners think to post on their social media accounts. Remember, even old people post pictures and videos." He also asked about the gun, "Could it have been purchased by someone and given to Alison or purchased by someone like her husband and taken by Alison when she went away for the weekend? Just thinking out loud."

He turned to his pile of party noise complaints and made a series of calls to the owners that complained. These owners had all complained about the noise from the Party House and other party houses in the RP Community. Maybe sitting down with Janey might be a good idea. She seemed to know almost everything that was going on in the Community. Janey could show him where the skeletons were buried. Brad thought she probably knew a lot more than Duke did.

He walked into Janey's office and said, "The food at the Cote d'Azur restaurant was outstanding. We made the reservation in time, and the owner and his wife greeted us like we were family. The waiters had been expecting us and made the evening wonderful. Kate was really impressed. The Dover Sole was outstanding. and the scallops were to die for. Thanks for recommending it." Brad changed the subject after she told him that she was glad they enjoyed the restaurant. "Janey, I wonder if you could take a few moments and talk to me about all these party complaints," he said.

Janey began to give him some real insight into the whole party scene. She told him that at one time Vic had a leasehold interest in thirty residences in RP with titles to the houses held by Smith, the developer of RP. As these were eventually sold by Smith, the new owner had an option to continue leasing the properties to Vic or take physical occupancy and end the lease. The Party House was acquired by Smith's project manager for the construction of RP, Jason Burns and Jason chose to continue the lease arrangement with Vic. Jason was OK with the party atmosphere and used it as a marketing device to sell homes in RP and in other projects in the area. There were other connections between Vic, the Party House, RP, and Smith's company, she noted.

She also told Brad that with the turnover to the Community by the developer, a new board from the Community was formed. One of their chief tasks was to negotiate a settlement of all issues between the Community and the developer. At issue were loans from the developer to pay multiple charges incurred by the developer to finish the project. The new Board of RP had selected three of their members to take charge of the negotiations and work with Duke to reach a settlement with Smith. Janey thought that Smith and his project manager began inviting the three directors in charge of the negotiations to parties at the Party House shortly after their appointment by the board. She thought that Smith believed that inviting them to the Party House from time to time would make the negotiations easier to conduct. She thought that the directors were impressed by the beauty of the guests and would not think to ask too many questions about them.

Brad asked, "Such as?"

Janey said, "Well, if these were guests at homes in the community, how were there so many? Don't we have a limit on the number of guests from a household? Obviously, no one is enforcing that. These guests could use any of the Club facilities on an unlimited basis. That included the Pool Bar, the Clubhouse restaurant, tennis, golf, and the spa and fitness center. Where were the owners? They were not at the Party House. No, these directors were looking at the beauty of the guests and the free flowing booze. They were not thinking that owners could not get to play a round of golf or get into an aerobics class."

Brad listened to all this and then Janey said, "Please don't mention that you heard any of this from me."

"I understand" said Brad. Brad wondered why the owners were not outside the Clubhouse with pitchforks and torches. Sometimes change happened from the top down, but in other cases it came from the bottom up. An outside force or influencer can stir things up and the top and the bottom become intertwined, much like a glass of iced tea responds to a spin of a long spoon. "Maybe my report will do that for RP," thought Brad. "I will just have to be careful how I say I learned all of this."

Chapter Twenty-One

Detective Cross: The Coroner Said What?

Detective George poked his head in Cross's office first thing Monday and began talking before he sat down in the chair in front of the desk. "The coroner's report is final now. It confirms the theory that the two victims shot each other and that the gunshot from the gun was the cause of death in each case. But there is a wrinkle in that report. Vance's body showed two anomalies that were not noticed at the time of the preliminary examination: first, there was a deep gash near the back of his head caused by a narrow blunt instrument, maybe a rod or stick but something hard, and second, there was a deep bruise on the underside of Vance's right forearm, probably from the same instrument. The reconstruction of the death is that Vance was struck in the head while in bed, found his gun, and before he was shot and killed was hit in the forearm by an ascending or backhand blow to his forearm. Whatever was used to strike Vance could have trace skin or hair. Nothing like that was found in the bedroom or the house. Finally, the techs, in completing their examination, reported that the gun used by Alison had traces of a lubricant used to clean and lubricate firearms and that traces of this same lubricant were found on Alison's right hand. That pretty much is icing on the cake. Clearly, Alison had the gun in her hand. The gunshot residue on her hand and body we think proves she fired the shot that killed Vic Vance. But nothing is ever easy, Cross", he said. He paused and continued, "On the table in the hallway between Vance and Alison's bedroom, the same lubricant was found. From the position of the lubricant on the table, we can only conclude that the gun was laying there before or at some time during the time she walked from her bedroom to Vance's room. Following that information, we reinterviewed Kaleisha Campbell. She was certain no gun was ever laying on the table at any time. She supervised the cleaning of the house daily and is absolutely certain that the only gun Vance had was in his room and kept in the drawer of the nightstand by his bed. I prodded her about whether Alison had brought a gun with her in her personal belongings and she was adamant that it was highly unlikely. Kaleisha had carried in Alison's suitcase and that of Charlie and had emptied them into the drawers of the bureau in the room. No gun. Kaleisha then recalled that Alison's handbag was so sheik that it would barely fit a compact and comb, let alone a gun. Suppose it could have been in the car, but no lubricant was found anywhere."

Cross had listened intently to George's report and said, "Holy shit, someone else may have been there, hit Vance, and fled, probably has this blunt instrument and may even have brought the gun into the house. A lot of maybes. This just might not be over. Let's have our technicians look at the videos that Brad sent over."

"Officer Budd and the techies have been looking at them," said George, "and maybe we will know something later this morning."

"I want to see them when she is finished with her review," Cross added.

Chapter Twenty-Two

Brad: Internet Replay

Brad was sitting at his desk that Monday afternoon, working on a multipage security report for RP management and its board. He took a short break on the document and opened the internet and found the Fort Myers news update on the web. They were replaying the press meeting that Jake had held on Saturday. The news typically gave a summary of the top stories from the previous weekend unless there was a bigger story in the news cycle. He had almost memorized Jake's little speech by now, so he spent time looking at the background. Upstairs on the railing of the porch on the second story, he spotted something unusual. It was a bright yellow tarp or sheet or blanket hanging on some of the porch furniture. Wonder what that could be. Before he logged off the website, he checked to see where Jake lived. "Interesting," he thought. "It's not too far away from here."

He returned to his report. He was getting close to completing the first draft. A half an hour later he saved the document and pushed back from the desk and looked at his watch. He had about two hours before he was meeting Kate for dinner. She was getting her hair done at the salon called Vanetta's which she had been talking about for days. Brad knew that these things usually took longer than estimated so he thought he could squeeze in a run. Maybe he could run along the river and see what Jake's condo looked like. He did not think it was more than four or five miles east of RP. The distance might even be shorter if he followed the river or found a path through the wooded area adjacent to the river. He would just have to be careful of the critters that called the area their homeland.

He always carried a set of running clothes with him when he went to work, and this assignment was not going to change that. He ducked into the restroom and changed; slipped his wallet, keys, and phone in a fanny pack; and set out the front gate to find the shortest route to Jake's condo. As he pounded the bike trail, he thought about the video. He had seen that color pattern he had seen on the porch before. This may be a waste of a good run. He didn't even know whose porch that was above Jake when he was giving his Oscar award winning monologue. At least he could work out a few kinks in his legs before hearing about the new hair styles Kate had considered before getting her hair done exactly like it already was.

He found that the bike trail crossed over the river to the southern bank and continued for several miles more. This was a terrific place to train either for running or with a bike, he thought. About one hundred yards after crossing the bridge over the river, he noticed a path that ran east into the woods. Clearly, this was used regularly by trail runners and hikers. There were city and park signs admonishing runners and hikers to respect the environment and not to litter or damage or injure the wildlife. Good advice, he thought. He slowed down his run to a jog then to a walk, and proceeded on the trail, keeping the riverbank to his left. About two and a half miles on the trail, he came to the side of a condo that looked like the one in Jake's video. He stopped momentarily, thinking, "What is the plan? Just circle the building and take a look around?" That sounded good. He resumed the run, circling counter clockwise around the building. When he reached the front of the building, he noticed the name of the complex as the Riverview which rang a bell from the newscast and confirmed by his internet search. Yes, this was the place. He looked up at the railing of the porch and saw nothing there now. "Guess I will not know what it was after all. Well, might as well make the circle and head back," he thought. He turned to the back side of the building and saw two things that were interesting. First, there was a paved walkway to the river and a launch point for watercrafts similar to the RP water recreational site. Had to be a good marketing point for the condo complex. The second was a set of dumpsters. He noticed that they had a critter lock on each that kept large animals from just lifting the lid and climbing in or spilling garbage all over the parking lot. They worked for raccoons and even bears in some cases. He had heard of these but had never seen one. He stopped and flipped the safety switch and opened up each dumpster and peered in, thinking that this would be a good device for the RP dumpsters as well. As he looked in the second dumpster, he noticed that at the bottom was the bright yellow material that he had seen in the video. He did not want to retrieve it, but he knew for certain what it was. It was an inflatable one-person kayak. He had seen one down at the beach in his first day at Fort Myers. This could have been used to float down the river and paddle back silently day or night. "Maybe this could have been the way our dark clothed intruder gained access to RP Friday night." He decided to call Detective George and tell him what he had found at the bottom of the dumpster.

Brad got home ahead of Kate, showered, and waited until the garage door opened. Kate came in and showed off her brandnew style that Vanetta had designed. He had to agree it looked great. He pretended to be eager to run his fingers through the new hairdo, and Kate acted in horror. Laughing she said, "Don't you dare. We are going out to dinner in thirty minutes with Duke and Robin, and I want to show off my new Florida hairstyle."

He sat down and updated her on all that he had been working on since he arrived. He said to her, "A lot of what will be in my report are simple findings that Duke had raised in our first conversation, and some of this just fell into my lap after I arrived. But my antennae are out though. I wonder if I was brought here as a smoke screen to cover up something else. I am concerned I cannot see it through all the smoke, and it is there right in front of my face. Maybe I rushed through this review and left issues on the table. I guess I will never know. Let's go to dinner."

As they were driving over to the Davidsons's house, Kate said, "I was visiting with Robin, and she showed me the new landscaping work that had been done around their property. It was an expensive job." Then as they were pulling into the Davidson's driveway, Kate mentioned, "You know that Duke and Robin met at one of the parties at the Party House?" Kate always had a way of taking Brad's breath away.

Chapter Twenty-Three
Dumpster Dive: Closing In

Detective George finished the call with Brad and thought, "This Brad guy is really interesting." He called in Officer Budd and briefed her, and they drove out to the Riverview condo in an unmarked police vehicle. This might be a wild goose chase, but there were still loose ends, and the mysterious golf course skulker was one of them. A few minutes later they parked in front of the dumpsters, got out, and looked in each. They began videotaping and photographing as they reached in, grabbed the kayak, and pulled it out. They looked again and saw a beige backpack containing a paddle and a pump at the bottom and grabbed that as well. Again, all was meticulously recorded. No identification was found in the pack or visible on the rubber kayak. They tagged each item and loaded them in the trunk of the car. They left as silently as they had come. Forensics and the other techies had more work to do.

The paddle was not strong enough to have made the blows to Vance's head or arm, so there was nothing to conclude about that. The techies found traces of gun lubricant in the bottom of the backpack. It matched the lubricant on Alison's hands and the gun she fired. They took her phone and did a deep dive into the various websites that she had visited in the last few months. There it was: an Amazon purchase of an inflatable one-person kayak, bright yellow marking with a beige backpack to carry the pump, paddle, and kayak. Things were coming together. Jake could have been there, but what did that mean?

Budd, George, and Cross got on a call with Brad when he got into the office Tuesday morning. He had planned to complete his report and deliver it to Duke that afternoon. "Could you come to Police Headquarters and chat this morning?" Cross asked. Brad said he could be there by ten A.M. He gave Duke the draft of the report and told him he needed to visit with the police about the car thieves and other security issues and would be back in the afternoon. Duke thanked him for the report and promised to read it before Brad returned. As Brad was packing his paperwork away and straightening out the office, Janey came into his office with the facilities manager, Rod Gomez, who he had met a few days earlier. She said that Rod knew he had been working on the Vance killing and the whole Party House mess and came to talk with her. As a result they both felt there were some things that he needed to know before he was finished with his work on the security report. Brad said he had just about finished looking at the areas of major concern but would be happy to sit down with them either tomorrow or when he got back from a meeting with the police. They nodded, but Janey said something curious, "We don't think you are quite done looking at the major issues, and we would ask that you don't mention to Duke about us wanting to meet with you."

"OK," he said. "Tomorrow then," and he left.

When Brad arrived at Cross's office, Cross thanked him for coming. Then he walked him to a conference room where Budd and George were waiting. After they all sat down, Cross said that Brad's suggestions and investigations had opened up their eyes to a broader picture of what must have happened to Vance and Alison Friday night.

Cross said, "The kayak could have been used to ferry a person down to the RP landing. There is evidence that a craft did pull into the beach landing at RP and was dragged ashore into the trees, as you found out for us. A person, consistent with the timeline, walks on the golf course and passes a house near the so called 'Party House' going in the direction of the Vance home. There is no real barrier between the property and Palm Tree Reserve. The distance between the boat landing and the Vance house could be walked in 15-30 minutes.

Again, this is consistent with the timeline. No entry could have been made from the main entrance to Palm Tree Reserve but could have been made by foot from the direction of the RP property. The rear door of the Vance house was accessible through the rear sliding door which showed no signs of being jimmied and according to Kaleisha was rarely locked. It is then possible that another person could have entered the house, entered into Vance's bedroom, and struck Vance in the head. Vance then finds his handgun and attempts to kill the intruder. He aims, and a second blow is struck by the intruder, knocking the arm off aim. The gun goes off, and Alison is hit as she enters the room with a gun that she picked up off the table. Whether she is ai ming at Vance or the intruder makes little difference, but she hits Vance center mass and kills him. The intruder panics and runs back to the kayak and paddles home to Riverview. We also believe that the gun that Alison fired was carried in the backpack found in the dumpster to the Vance home and left on the hall table. We believe it was picked up and used by Alison to shoot Vance. We can show that an inflatable kayak like the one found in the dumpster was purchased by Alison some time before the events in question. So we believe we can place Jake with a kayak and a backpack like the one found in the dumpster. He has access to the river, and material like the kayak can be seen in the news video on the balcony to Jake's condo. We plan to obtain a subpoena to search Jake's condo and car to see if there is any other evidence that can be found. None of this alters the cause of death of Vance and Alison but does demonstrate that, but for the involvement of this golf course stalker, both Vance and Alison might be alive. And frankly, Brad, but for your nosing around, we would have known none of this. It is likely though we may never be successful in prosecuting Jake for this unless more evidence is discovered." Cross said further, "There is nothing more that you should or can do, Brad, but we wanted to express our thanks for your efforts. Just watch the news stations over the next few days. Maybe we will find something more." Brad thanked Cross and his team and had planned to return to his office. But as he was driving to RP, he got a call on his cell. He looked down at the phone mounted in the cup holder of the car and, not recognizing the number, let it roll over to voicemail. When it was safe to pullover, he stopped and listened to the message. It was Janey and Rod. They wanted to talk tonight and, if possible, out of the office. He called the number back and talked to both of them and suggested they come to his house around eight P.M. They said fine but that it would be best if the conversation could take place outside on the lanai rather in the house. "Well, it is going to be nice tonight, and that sounds like a good idea. See you then." He thought, "Wow, that was a strange conversation,"

Chapter Twenty-Four
Files And Videos: Could It Be?

Brad and Kate ate a simple meal, and Brad brought her up to date on the review. He said Janey and Rod Gomez would be there at eight P.M. and he felt certain that whatever they intended to say to him probably involved managers and maybe directors of RP. He was wrong.

Janey and Rod parked their cars around the block from Brad and Kate's house, and instead of coming to the front door, they walked around the side of the house to the lanai and sat down around the patio table. Brad had been waiting in the kitchen when he heard the patio chairs scraping the floor of the lanai. He grabbed a cup of coffee from the kitchen counter and walked out and sat down at the patio table. Rod looked at Janey and then turned to Brad and spoke, "We know all the dirt that you have been finding and felt if we did not talk to you now, it might be the last opportunity we had to do so. You have to understand that we are really afraid that talking with you like this will at least jeopardize our positions with RP or worse." Janey nodded as Rod finished speaking.

"I will do my best to keep this confidential," Brad said.

"There is a pretty good chance that Duke knows we are here. We think there are listening devices in this house and in your office at work," Janey said. Brad blinked twice and said, "Well let's proceed. If we act fast, we can stay ahead of trouble and work to resolve what is wrong."

Rod began. "I assume you have been to Duke's house and sat by his beautiful pool." Brad nodded. "Well, the pool was put in three months ago by a contractor of the Smith Company, the developer of RP. This was installed at no charge to Duke. The costs for the pool are included in the charge backs Smith is seeking to recover in the negotiations to resolve all turn over issues. These charge backs are being treated by Smith as a loan by RP and the loans details. The accounts supporting the loans include the cost of Duke's pool. It is unlikely that this will never see the light of day. But I have a copy of the pool contractor's $75,000 bill and the accounting entry by the developer into the chargeback account. We found on the Postbook social media account of the pool contractor a picture from one of the recent Party House events. There, on the posting is a picture of Duke, the pool contractor, Smith, Vic Vance, and several of the female party guests. This was posted a week before you arrived to begin your work, Brad."

Janey interrupted and said, "But wait, there is more. Rod found out that our grounds crew was sent to Duke's house after the pool was completed and brought a truck load of trees, shrubs, ground cover, and other landscaping materials to fully landscape the pool area and the front of Duke's house. While these were Club personnel doing the work, the plantings are estimated to have been about $7,500. It was buried in the landscaping purchases for that month. When I asked our landscape foreman Pete about it, he said Robin had set the project up, designating the precise plantings and materials and oversaw the work by Pete's crew. This was not a disposal of excess or surplus materials that could not have been returned to the supplier if unneeded. This was deliberate. This was planned. This was wrong."

"This sounds pretty bad," said Brad. "I assume that the pool and the trees are just part of why you are here."

Janey resumed the story, "We found other Postbook pictures from the party that the pool contractor attended at the Party House. We noticed in the background that three of the servers from the RP Pool Bar could be seen waiting on guests. We talked to the Pool Bar manager yesterday, and he confirmed that Duke routinely authorized three or four servers to report to Vance's house for big weekend parties. The servers did not complain because they were paid by the Club, and the tips were unseemly. But the Pool Bar manager admitted that the understanding was that all tips the servers received were to be split with the Pool Bar manager and Duke." Janey had no idea how much had passed hands because it was all in cash. But the scam had been going on for months according to Janey.

Janey said, "I talked to Johnnie, one of the servers, about all this, and he confirmed that he was forced to share his tips from the Party House. He was happy with the amount of the tips he was pocketing but felt guilty getting paid by RP and working at the Party House. He said he would share any information that might be of interest to me."

Rod ran the anchor leg of their relay telling Brad the rest of the story. "Well, we know from your report," he began.

"What, you saw my report?" shouted Brad.

Janey said, "Yes, a copy was left on the printer when you went to see the police." Brad relaxed.

Rod continued, "You know that Smith has been trying to influence several of the directors in the negotiations of the loans related to project charge backs. The invitations to these three directors to parties at the Party House and setting them up with beautiful women was only part of it. Incidentally, Brad, these three directors were appointed at the recommendation of Duke to the turnover financial review committee. Duke and this committee have signed off on the entire financial chargeback account and are prepared to recommend a settlement number at the Board meeting tomorrow. Once I found the pool charges, I asked Janey to look over the entire ledger with me. We have looked through the entire ledger and found entries totaling $100,000 in payments to these directors and Duke. Of course they are not blatantly obvious but were in the form of home improvements, payment of real estate taxes, and long-term vehicle leases. The developer knows how to bury things, but we found them. We think that the developer has overstated the chargeback account by at least a million dollars, not including the payments that Duke and the others have received."

Janey said, "Sorry to dump this on you Brad, but everything is coming down tomorrow, and this is our last ditch stand before we just hold our noses and let it pass."

Janey said, "One more thing. I got a copy of a video that Johnnie sent me Saturday. It was shot by him while at the party Friday night at the Party house. It shows Duke huddled with the directors of the turnover financial review committee and Smith giving each other high fives and handshakes and walking off with female party guests upstairs to the guest bedrooms." She had run the video on her smart phone as she was narrating.

Brad said, "I think you made your case. This race is over; you have lapped the field. If you excuse me, I have to redo the report. Then I have a board meeting to prepare for. Give me your files and the electronic photos and videos, and I will take it from here."

In about two hours he had taken the report he had given Duke earlier that day and updated it with all of the revelations he had received from Janey and Rod and prepared a five-page executive summary, about one tenth of the length of the entire report. He called the President and Chair of the Board, Stosh Salinski, at seven A.M. Wednesday morning and asked to see him.

CHAPTER TWENTY-FIVE

"Really It Is"

Stosh agreed to meet Brad at a coffee shop near Walmart about a mile from RP. Brad brought a tablet with him on which he had downloaded both his presentation and the videos and photos he had gathered during his review. As they were sitting down, NBC2 began airing a news update on the TV monitor above their heads. Ashley Moran reported that police had conducted a search of Jake Reynold's condo and found a weapon that was used in connection with the home invasion of Vic Vance's house and that implicated him is the deaths of both Vance and Reynold's wife, Alison. Police reported that Jake had made admissions to the police during a tearful confession.

Brad could only shake his head. He turned to Stosh and said: "Duke asked me to conduct a review of the security conditions of RP and make some recommendations. They are detailed in a report I have addressed to the Board. Here is a copy for you in advance. It covers security cameras, fence improvements, steps that the owners need to do in assuming self-accountability, and other issues that will sound like common sense. But the bottom line is that the Board needs to take control of this community, set the rules that the owners can live by, and reasonably enforce them. Finally, you need to make sure that the GM works for you and not the other way around."

Stosh sat there stunned and asked, "What do you mean?" Brad then showed Stosh a video of one of the parties at the Party

House which showed Duke and the three directors on the turnover finance committee drinking and partying with the developer Smith and Jason, the Smith project manager. He then pushed a spreadsheet report of an internal financial review of the charges supporting Smith's loans to RP relating to construction charge backs. They showed an overcharge of over a million dollars, illegal payments, and benefits to each of these three directors, Bogatus, Renquist, and North cross, well in excess of $100,000 and improper services and payments to Duke and his family in excess of $80,000. Brad said, "These call into question the validity of the settlement agreement that I understand is being presented later today at the board meeting. At the least, an independent audit of the accounts should be performed, and all three directors should be disciplined." Then Brad said, "Look, I have had a cordial relationship with Duke, and I have come to really like the guy. But if any of this is verified, I cannot see how your board could have him stay. In reality, the three board members; Duke; maybe his wife, Robin; Smith; and several of his employees could be indicted for theft and fraud and other felonies. You will have to deal with Duke sooner rather than later. All that I have just said and given to you is in a report that I intend to share with the Fort Myers District Attorney because they involve criminal conduct by members of your board and your GM. I wanted to give you the first crack at dealing with this before I do. In light of what I have just said, I want to tell you I will not be attending the board meeting but will be leaving today. Here is my bill for services and expenses." He gave Stosh a nod and left him there with the tablet and the original of the report, keeping the report to the DA for later transmittal.

He called Kate from the car and said, "We need to pack and head back home. The project is over, and I don't think we will be welcome here much longer. By the way, I have booked our flight and we have time for one last swim at the beach."

Later, as they were driving to the airport, he heard the radio report the following:

"Stosh Salinski, the President and chair of the RP board of directors announced today in an electronic message to the owners of RP that the board of directors of RP had accepted the resignations of three of its board members, Messers Bogatus, Renquist, and Northcross, and its GM, Duke Davidson. He also announced that the board had asked Janey Boothe to assume the role of GM and the hiring of Ralph Donald as the full-time security director."

Shortly thereafter there was an exclusive report from ABC7's Petrof Manheim that the developer of River Palms, Sean Smith, was arrested for fraud and illegal payments.

Brad and Kate were already planning the next Ironman race. Maybe Iron-man Florida or even back to Coeur d'Alene!